Flirts! 5 Romantic Short Stories

Lisa Scott

DEDICATION

To my perpetually single friend G.G. who has inspired
many of my short stories. The Hot Girl's Friend?
That's me. And she's the hot girl everyone always asks
me about. And she's even prettier on the inside.

CONTENTS

ACKNOWLEDGMENTS

Thanks to my family for their constant support and
understanding. Writing requires a lot of solo time.
They never complain.

"The Hot Girl's Friend"
By Lisa Scott

A night out with Miranda always ended in
one of two ways: either she found this week's love
of her life right off the bat and I caught an early
cab home for a night of popcorn and bad cable
reality shows; or I spent the entire evening fending
off the smitten males whose pheromones went on
high alert the moment her big toe entered the
room.

This night was going in the direction of option
number two. I didn't see any hot prospects at first
glance. McGinty's Bar was the place to be in
Springfield, Massachusetts on a Saturday night.
The place was packed with the crowd spilling
onto the back patio to enjoy the warm summer
night, and the music was thumping at a gotta-
shout level. All eyes turned to the door when she
walked in. A path cleared as six-foot-tall Miranda,
platinum-blond hair hanging past her curvy hips,
wiggled her way onto the dance floor.

I followed, because she couldn't get her
groove on without me. I'm a better dancer than
she is and she steals all her moves from me. It's
true. I've got that going for me, at least—not that
anyone notices her five-foot-four, dark-haired
friend with the thick ankles. Her shadow certainly
swallows me whole, but hey, not everyone wants
to be in the spotlight. Suits me just fine.

We boogied to the hip song of the moment,

2

and, soon enough, a few gutsy gals left the security of the scattered tables and joined us. Then the drunker of the men crowded the floor, probably wondering if they should shoot for the top and approach Miranda or pick one of us "lesser" girls—like they could flatter us into bed by flirting with us first. For the most part, men at bars are idiots. Newsflash, I know.

"You with the hot chick?" a short, curly-haired guy asked, bumping his hip into mine in some pretence of a dance move.

I bumped back hard enough that he had to catch his balance. "If you mean the tall blond, yes, I am."

Out came another bad dance move, with him jiggling his hands like he was shaking a Martini. "She available?"

I shook my head and gave him the bad news. "Not exactly. She starts her prison sentence tomorrow. This is kind of a last hurrah."

His bushy eyebrows scrunched as he recalculated his plan of attack, not quite ready to give up the chase. Perhaps prison stripes are a turn-on for some guys.

I shrugged. "I suppose she could use a pen pal. Although her ex might be writing to her, too. He seems to have gotten over the whole stabbing thing. You really only *need* one testicle, right?" I boogied away from him and started getting my excuses ready for the string of men who would soon be lining up to meet the second most appealing woman in the bar—the hot chick's best friend. Always a good girl to know when trying to make your move. At least, that's what the men

3

seemed to think.

A group of college guys had separated me from Miranda, but she seemed to be enjoying herself in-between two of them, so I made my way over to the bar and collapsed on a stool.

The bartender came over and I asked for a Coke. Bras dangled in a rainbow of hues and sizes from a crisscross of beams above him. We'd been there before and I was surprised Miranda hadn't added to the collection. Not me, though. Bras are expensive, and with a good-sized chest myself, I didn't usually go walking around without one. I'm classy like that.

"Not drinking tonight?" the bartender asked.

"I need to keep my wits about me." I grinned at him. He was cute, with wavy brown hair tucked behind his ears and bright blue eyes. Then he smiled, revealing dimples I could take a bath in. That earned him an immediate upgrade to hot. I wished I were wearing something nicer than a black mini-skirt and a tank top.

He nodded in Miranda's direction. "You with the blonde? Does she want a drink?"

I sighed. *She's man-nip even on the other side of the room.* "Alcohol doesn't mix well with her medication, and considering how contagious she is, we don't want to mess with the meds."

He snapped his bar towel at me. "I'm not interested in your friend. I just thought I'd hook you both up with a drink since you're sitting here and there's no line."

I took my purse off my shoulder and set it on the bar. "That's a new one. Not interested in

4

Miranda. Never heard that one before."

Shaking his head, he left to get my soda. It didn't take long for the first poor chap to find me. He was skinny and tall with shaggy blond hair covering his eyes. "Hey, that girl you're with?" He shoved his hands in his pockets as I admired his highlights.

I cocked my head as if confused. "Which girl?"

He pointed to Miranda's golden head sticking up above the crowd. "That one. The blonde. What's her deal? She single?"

I crossed my legs and looped my hands around my knee. "I guess you could say she's single. But her court-ordered therapist has forbidden her from dating men for a while, otherwise, it's back to county lockup." I shrugged. "But you never know, she might bend the rules. Just don't give her your real name. It's really hard to change your identity if things don't work out."

"Uh, thanks." He scratched his head and walked to the opposite end of the bar, stealing a glance over his shoulder at Miranda.

"I'm disappointed."

I jumped, surprised to find the bartender leaning towards me with my drink. I was so busted, but I could play innocent just as well as I could lie. I widened my eyes. "Disappointed? In the weather? Your stock portfolio?"

He slid my glass to me. "His excuse was much more clever than mine."

My eyes narrowed. "Maybe if I knew you'd be eavesdropping tonight, I would have come up with something better for you." I snagged a few cherries from the fruit tray in front of him and dropped them in my Coke.

He gestured to the tray. "Do help yourself to the salad bar."

"That's the plan. I like to be fancy." I bounced my foot the beat of the music.

He bent down, reappeared with a pink drink umbrella, and stuck it in between the ice cubes. "There you go. You're the fanciest girl in the bar. I just hope they provide your poor friend with her medication when she's in county lockup." He rubbed his chin in mock concern.

"Oh, they do. Medical care in prison is much better than the plan I've got." I twirled the umbrella between my fingers. "I think they even give her double doses."

He propped his elbows on the shiny, black bar top. "How do you know she wouldn't have wanted to meet that nice young man? He might have lovely eyes under that hair."

I stabbed the umbrella back in between the ice cubes. "Don't worry. Miranda finds the ones she's interested. I keep the rest out of her way."

"How kind of you. And she wouldn't object to these inspired excuses you're using?" He ignored the two men standing next to me, waiting for a drink.

I reached in my purse, fished out my favorite Mac lip gloss, and applied a coat. "She thinks it's hilarious. I tell her all about them at the end of the night and she picks her favorite. We've been friends for a long time. If I didn't love her so much, I'd hate her." I rubbed my lips together, enjoying the cinnamon zing.

"You two grow up together?"

He was ruining my fun. "Not exactly."

He looked at me, waiting for an explanation.

"That's a long story for another night."

He held up his hands. "I'm here every weekend."

"I'll jot that down in my planner." *Really, I will.* "But let's just say we both have very good reasons for my being her social director."

He frowned at the growing drink line, held up one finger in a just-a-second gesture, and got the guys their drinks. Then he came back to me. "What's your name, guardian of the beautiful Miranda?"

I laughed. "Jane Jameson."

He held out his hand. "Brady Flynn. Pleased to meet you."

I shook his hand and a shiver shot down to my toes. Damn, this guy was cute, and those strong hands were certainly capable of more interesting things than serving beer to clowns at a bar.

Unfortunately, contestant number two approached before we could finish talking. I sighed dramatically. *I should just hold up a sign that says, "She's not available."*

The guy leaned up against the bar next to me. "Can I buy you a drink?"

Oh, very nice—the old bait and switch routine. I'll pretend I'm interested in you and then make a move on your friend. "Sure, I was just about to order a Johnny Walker Black. A double, straight up." He was wearing Hollister jeans; he could afford it.

7

His eyes bulged, but he nodded to Brady, who turned around, stifling a laugh.

"Thanks," I told the guy. He was tall and well built with a cute goatee, and might have had a shot with Miranda if not for the tongue piercing. There were certain body parts she considered sacred. The tongue was one of them so this guy was out of the running.

Brady returned with my drink, which I let sit on the counter.

Mr. Bait-and-Switch went in for the kill. "So, what can you tell me about your friend?"

I blinked at him a few times. "Who?"

He gave me a look. "Blondie out there. I saw you come in with her. What's her deal?"

I widened my eyes. "Oh, my gosh! Are you interested?"

Trying to hold back a smile, he fingered his goatee. "Well, yeah. Sure."

"You're just her type." I clapped and squealed, bouncing my feet on the rungs of the barstool. "She's going to be so excited. They just let her out of the facility." I reached for his arm. "She hasn't been out in the general population for what, four years now? Be careful with her."

He pulled his arm away and stepped back. "Maybe it's not the best time for her right now."

"Really?" I pouted. "Darn it."

He eyed the drink he'd bought me and then wandered away. Brady leaned over the bar so his mouth was right next to my ear. "Why not just say she has a boyfriend?" His breath was hot on my cheek.

I turned to him, falling in love all over again.

8

"Because then they try even harder."

One corner of his mouth quirked up. "Why not say she's your girlfriend?"

I cocked an eyebrow. "Then they're even more interested."

He laughed. "Must be hard, coming up with so many reasons."

I plucked a cherry from my Coke and popped it in my mouth. "Not really. Sometimes I try to keep a theme to my excuses. Like tonight they might all have a criminal element. That'd be fun. Or maybe I'll stick with the medical and mental excuses." I rubbed my hands together as I tried to decide.

He wiped down the bar and shook his head. "A woman with a PhD in lying. Impressive. Need a refill or will you be enjoying the top-shelf whiskey you stuck that poor chump with?"

"Lying for a good cause doesn't count as lying. It's creative protection." I patted the bar top. "And keep the whiskey there, it makes me look sophisticated, right?"

"Next to the Coke with an umbrella and five cherries? Definitely."

"Thought so." I looked for Miranda in the crowd. She had moved on from the college boys and was now dancing with a tall, redheaded guy. He didn't stand a chance. She'd crossed redheaded guys off her list months ago. Currently, she was looking for someone Australian — since she'd never had the pleasure — or someone with yacht, since she *had* had that pleasure and wanted to enjoy it again. That's when I saw another guy making a beeline for me.

9

I swore under my breath.

"Hey, how you doing?"

I smiled. "I'm a little itchy, actually." I scratched the back of my neck. "A bit sweaty, too. I have a terrible headache. And cramps." I grimaced and set my hand on my tummy. "How are you?"

He blinked at me a few times and then looked over at Miranda. "I'd be a lot better if I was leaving with *her*. You're her friend, right? What's her 411?"

Brady leaned between us. "Isn't she back together with Gino?"

I looked backed at him, smiled and nodded. "Impressive," I mouthed.

Brady scanned the crowd. "I swear I saw him tonight. Hard to miss a two-hundred-fifty-pound guy."

I tapped my finger against my nose. "Are you sure he's out of jail already?"

"I think so."

I shook my head. "It's amazing how low bail is for breaking a guy's arm just for pinching his girlfriend's ass."

The guy slowly backed away.

"Give it a shot. I'm not sure if they're back together or not," I said.

His Adam's apple bounced in his throat. "Thanks. I'm all set."

I turned around and high-fived Brady. "Nice work."

"Thank you, thank you. I only hope she provides you the same courtesy when losers come looking for you."

That earned him a steely gaze. "You think I can only attract losers?'

He groaned and looked up at the ceiling and all those bras. "You know what I mean. A guy with a lame line, like the yahoos here."

Frowning, I rolled my eyes. "It's never really been a problem."

"Oh, only the A-plus specimens show up for you?"

I looked away. "Knock it off."

"What?" He reached for my arm and I pulled it away.

"Come on, I don't look like Miranda." I gestured to her waving her hands over her head in the middle of a group of hot Latino men. Only a girl as confident as her could do that in a strapless dress. "I don't exactly have guys banging down the door." Or knocking at all. It had been a while.

Another guy interrupted us. "Hey, you friends with the hot chick?"

I pointed at Brady. "That's her boyfriend. He can tell you all about her."

The guy held up his hands and stepped back. "Sorry, dude."

"No problem. She's a hot mess anyway. You don't want any of that action."

He was gone before Brady could finish.

I flicked a cherry stem at him. "Stop it. Anybody would want her."

"Oh, my God." He dropped his head back in frustration. "You seriously believe that's all guys are interested in? Looks?"

I turned up my hands like, yeah duh.

He let out a long sigh. "Come on, Jane. We're

not all Neanderthals."

"Yes, you are. I think your bra collection says it all." I jerked my chin toward the lingerie.

"I've never actually collected one myself. See? Not one of the bad guys."

I pressed my eyes closed before launching into my theory on men. "I just mean its hardwired into your brain, or chemistry, or whatever, to look for the most attractive female mate. Haven't you ever read those studies about men preferring a certain hip-to-waist ratio, which happens to be the most fertile ratio? Then there's the clear skin and shiny hair that suggest good, healthy genes. You can't help it. It's in your nature to want the most attractive mate who'll best be able to spread your seed." I took a long drink. "And for that reason, no man would ever pick me over Miranda. She is reproductive perfection." A little drama always helped sell it, so I spread my arms wide. "It's not your fault."

By this time, Brady was pinching the bridge of his nose, shaking his head. "You are wrong."

"And you must be drunk. I thought bartenders weren't allowed to drink on the job." I stood up and leaned over the bar, pretending to search for a contraband beverage.

A giggling brunette wearing too much dark, eye shadow sidled up next to me and waved to get Brady's attention. "Excuse me, my friend over there was wondering if you're single?" She pointed to a girl covering her face with both hands; but there was no question whether or not the short, chubby girl with frizzy red hair was a looker. Being a non-goddess myself, I was allowed to make such judgment calls.

The brunette giggled a bit more. "She thinks you're hot. If you want, she'll give you her bra for your collection." She pointed to the lingerie and slapped her hand over her mouth, totally overwhelmed with how audacious she was being.

I tried to suppress my grin, watching how Brady would handle this one.

He tilted his head and shrugged. "Man, sometimes it really sucks having a girlfriend." He reached for a wine glass, and poured some Chardonnay. "But give her this and tell her thanks for the compliment; and that she should keep her bra for some other lucky fellow."

The girl pouted, but she took the wine and dashed over to her friend.

"Very nicely done," I said.

He gave me a little bow, when someone tapped my shoulder. I turned around. "Yes?"

"Ah, 'allo love. I was wondering if you knew that lovely blond girl tearing about on the dance floor?" He had an accent that sounded British but wasn't exactly. Could it be the elusive Australian?

Now this is an interesting development. "I do know her. Say, you aren't Australian, are you?" Maybe I'd be getting out of here earlier than I expected.

He frowned at me. "No. If I were Australian I'd sound like an ass." He shuddered a bit as he said it. "I'm South African."

"Oh." I scrunched my eyebrows, trying to remember Miranda's status with the African nations. "Let me get back to you. You don't have a yacht, do you?"

He shook his head.

"A dinghy?"

He just looked at me and walked away.

"What the hell?" I mumbled. "I was going to ask her if she was interested. She's got a tour-of-the-nations thing going on."

Brady refilled my Coke and dropped in a handful of cherries. "Back to your *totally* plausible theory on men and our shallow evolutionary desires. If that's all we Neanderthals want is a beautiful woman—never mind smarts, or humor, or loyalty, or any of that business—what about you women? What do you want?"

"Simple." I shrugged. "Power and money to help raise all your children."

He laughed. "Then I'm in big trouble because I've got neither."

"Well, not all women want that. I suppose those of us who aren't evolutionary goddesses know we have to settle." I wasn't about to tell him that he was a Ryan Reynolds' look-alike and could get any woman in the bar. "As we just saw, you don't have a hard time with the ladies. How do you fend them off?"

"I tell them all I've got a girlfriend."

I tucked my hair behind my ears and prayed it wasn't frizzing. "Is that the truth or an excuse?"

He folded his arms and his expression turned serious. "I'll be honest with you to balance out your lying tonight. It's an excuse, because I typically don't like to swim in the dating pool that shows up here."

I set my hand in my chin and leaned forward,

intrigued. "Oh, and where do you go trolling for women?"

"I don't make it a point to look. I figure I'll find her when the time is right."

"And if Miranda came over and said she was interested in you? Would the time be right then?" I toyed with the zipper pull on my purse, not wanting to see the truth in his eyes.

He shrugged. "I don't even know her."

With the wave of my hand, I dismissed that ridiculousness. "Stop it. Of course you'd go out with her."

"Not necessarily. I might decide she was self-absorbed after a few minutes. And I'm not the only one." He refilled a beer and slid it to the man next to me, waiting.

"I think my results so far here tonight would prove otherwise."

"You're polling the wrong crowd. If you and Miranda went somewhere besides a bar, I bet there'd be plenty of guys asking her about you. Here at a bar, a six-foot-tall blond woman is like a bug light. She totally stands out, attracting all the creatures buzzing about at night. And they have no idea they're about to be zapped by you." He pointed at me and I thought about biting his finger.

I rolled my eyes instead. "She stands out everywhere."

He tipped his head and stared at me for a moment. I wondered if I'd forgotten to pluck my right eyebrow again. I fluffed my bangs and did a quick swipe for eye stubble. Phew. All clear.

"Do you always go out with her?" he

asked. "Everywhere?"

"Usually."

"Maybe Miranda's your excuse to keep guys away." He smiled, like he'd just come up with a great new As-Seen-On-TV invention.

I opened my mouth then snapped it shut. "I need a minute to think about that warped logic."

"You're not going to meet a nice guy at a bar. And certainly not with her in tow."

"Then good thing I have a cat at home who loves me, because most of the men I meet are at bars."

He planted both hands on the counter top. "Okay. You need to meet an entirely new population of men. You've been corrupted by losers. I've got a proposition. Come with me to my baseball game tomorrow—without Miranda— and we'll see how many guys are interested in you."

I tried to look incredibly offended. "Good Lord, you make me feel like chattel. Are you going to sell me to the highest bidder?"

"I'm just intent on proving your theory wrong. I'll bet you have a date in three weeks."

"Three weeks? You think it's going to take that long? Thanks."

He forced a great big smile for me. "No, I just imagine you're going to be very difficult about this."

"That's very true. But let's make a wager on this bet." I narrowed my eyes, thinking, and then snapped my fingers. "A t-shirt that says, "She's Taken." I can flash it at guys when they come up to ask about Miranda."

He shook his head. "Now, what good will that be for me when I win it? Because I will."

"I'll have it printed to say "I'm Taken" so you can use it when girls itching to lose their bras come up to you."

He reached over the bar to shake my hand. "Deal. And I wear a Large. Meet me at this address tomorrow at one." He scrawled directions to his baseball game on the back of a bar napkin as Miranda wandered over.

I picked up the glass of scotch. "Want some?" I asked her. "It's a double. You helped me get it."

She smoothed her hair and arched her head back, making her already long neck look like it belonged in a classy erotic photo display. "Can I have a glass of water?" She tucked her hair over one shoulder and smiled at Brady.

And he got her some water pretty damn fast.

"Who's your friend, Jane?" she asked, lowering her lashes.

No, not the coy voice! Not the lashes of lust! "This is Brady. Brady, this is my friend Miranda."

She reached over to squeeze the tips of his fingers. "Very nice to meet you."

"Bad news, he's not Australian and he doesn't have a yacht. I checked."

He laughed, and wiped the bar with his rag. "Plus, I have a girlfriend."

And didn't that make my heart sing?

She stuck out her bottom lip and turned to me. "In that case, I'm ready to go home. Are you, Jane?"

I hopped off the barstool. "You don't have to ask me twice."

17

She headed for the door, and I swiped the napkin from the bar.

"The medication making her sleepy?" Brady asked.

"Nah, it's a parole curfew."

Out came the dimples. "See you tomorrow."

"Only to prove you wrong." I smiled at him over my shoulder as we left.

*****

"Damn," Miranda said, climbing into the cab. "He was cute. He would've been fun."

I said nothing, annoyed for the first time that she could have whoever she wanted. *But Brady told her he was taken.* That made me squeal inside. "He's a bartender. Not your type." Normally, I supported any fling she was considering. She had very good reason to pack in as much fun as possible. I did my best to make sure she didn't get hurt in the process. It's a role I'd been playing for a while.

She leaned her head back against the seat while I tried to touch as little of the foul, plastic, peeling material on the seats as possible.

"So, what was your best excuse of the night?" she asked.

I tapped my fingers on my thigh, thinking, as the cab lurched through the city, the pine-tree air-freshener swinging on the rear view mirror. "Actually, Brady helped me out with a good one."

"The hot bartender knew what you were doing?"

"He overheard me. And I used one on him when he asked me if you'd want a drink. Told him it didn't mix with your meds."

She pretended to slug me. "Don't scare away the cute ones."

I threw up my hands. "What? I didn't think you'd be interested."

"I could be interested for a night or two."

"He's too nice for that."

She gave me a look. "Did someone finally catch your eye?"

I shook my head too hard. "No, he was just fun, helping me come up with excuses. We told one guy your boyfriend was in the bar—fresh out of jail."

She rested her head on my shoulder. "Oh, Janey, I do love you."

The cab pulled in front our apartment building. She lived across the hall from me in downtown Springfield. Which was like a zebra living in Idaho, really. Why she wasn't a model living in Boston or some other big city was beyond me. But she was quite content working as a kindergarten teacher with her summers off. Those poor little boys in her class would never find a woman who could live up to their first teacher crush. I'm sure there were a few smitten daddies, too, scheduling extra parent-teacher conferences.

"I'll be up around noon. Want to do lunch?" she asked.

I opened the door to the building. "Some of us have to work," I whispered.

"Oh, you're no fun."

"And you're all fun. We balance out."

"Add Brady to my list. If he's ever available, I'm in. We'll have to check back in a few weeks. Nighty-night, Janey. Love you." She blew me a kiss and let herself into her apartment.

Glad someone does. "Back at ya," I said.

*****

The only reason I tried on seven different outfits the next day was because of the flaky weather report. Sun, rain, hail—make up your mind, weather people. Plus, purple and blue both played up my eyes, but which to choose?

Mr. Mew just looked at me with his big yellow eyes, so he was no help. I went with blue and hoped for the best.

Not that it mattered what I was wearing, I decided, driving to the baseball field. Brady would be a good friend to have. Yep, just what a girl like me needed, another good looking guy friend. But I left my loose brown curls down, because sometimes they looked cute bouncing on my shoulders. Or so Miranda told me. And as much as I liked running around without makeup, I put on pale lipstick, eyeliner and mascara. I looked as good I could without appearing as though I'd tried. It's a hard balance to strike.

I was hoping Brady wouldn't be as hot in the daylight, so that maybe I could shake these feelings, but his tight white pants and McGinty's Bar t-shirt only made his assets more visible. I nodded in approval. Hopefully, he was friends with equally gorgeous men. The mythical ones, who valued personality and humor in a girl over looks. He was so losing this bet.

I waved to him when he spotted me leaning against the chain link fence surrounding the field. He was practicing with his teammates and tossed the ball to the guy on third base, then ran over, leaving a trail of red dust in his wake. I tried to remember the last time I'd made it to third base and I was coming up blank.

"You came," he said with a smile.

And that hasn't happened in a while either, I thought to myself. "Only to prove you wrong." I wrapped my fingers around the metal links.

"Nope, I think I'm going to have a new T-shirt to keep the ladies in line."

I tried to swat his arm but he ducked out of the way. "Go sit down and cheer for me. But don't get too hoarse. I'm awesome, you'll have lots of cheering to do."

"Clearly you awesome. You have to be, to make it to the bar league, right?"

"Try not to cut yourself with that sharp tongue. I don't have any band-aids on me." He shook his head, laughing, and ran onto the field.

Brady was good. He scored three runs, made a couple of key catches, and had a gaggle of girls waiting for him when it was all over. Shocker. But after some casual chitchat, he pushed his was past them and came over to me.

Yes, me: the only girl there wearing sneakers instead of high-heeled sandals, zero jewelry and a "Wanna Smurf Around" t-shirt.

"Impressive, as promised," I told him as he sat down next to me on the bleachers.

He jabbed his thumb over his shoulder. "We're heading to a pub down the street to celebrate our crushing victory."

He didn't have to say so, but I knew this is where he was going to put his theory to the test. I should have been nervous realizing I'd soon be trying to charm his friends with my wit and personality. But I knew it was going to lead nowhere, and being right was so much fun. Plus that "She's Taken" t-shirt would come in handy.

"It's close enough to walk. You ready?" he asked.

"Let's do it."

Eight of us sat at a big table, sharing wings and war stories from our high school sports careers. Or lack of a career in my case. "I'm just saying, how many concussions do you need to suffer on the volleyball court before you realize it's not your calling? The coaches pawned me off on each other until I finally gave up sports and joined the drama club. And they kicked me out for being too dramatic."

Brady's friend, Finn, just laughed and shook his head. "What kind of volley balls did you use? I remember them being very soft."

"True, but the floor was quite hard when the ball hit me and knocked me over."

Finn's eyes swept over me. "You should have moved on to beach volleyball. You certainly could handle the uniform." Up went a sexy eyebrow. "I could teach you a few moves this weekend. Bunch of us are hitting the beach on the South Shore if you're interested."

I almost ducked, hearing the flirty comment sail my way, like an errant volleyball. I looked over at Brady, expecting a told you so smirk, but he was frowning. "She can't make it." He scratched his head. "She just had a pre-cancerous mole removed. A great big one on her back. It was all hairy. And lumpy. She has to stay out of the sun unless she's totally covered up."

My mouth dropped open and I glared at him. Who did he think he was — *me*? And why was he shooing off the very men he'd been trying to set me up with? I excused myself to hit the restroom and jerked my head, signaling him to follow me.

As he caught up to me outside the bathroom, I pretended to fan myself. "Gosh, Mr. Quinn, how could I have forgotten my great big sunbonnet today to shield me from the venomous rays of the sun?" I crossed my arms. "And did you have to make the mole hairy? God. Did I miss the purpose of today's little exercise?" I tried to sound mad, but he flashed these puppy dog eyes at me that would undoubtedly get him out of any jam.

He grabbed my shoulders. "I know. I'm sorry. He definitely seemed interested, but he's no good for you."

I swatted away his hands. "I'll decide that for myself once I see if he has six pack abs or not. And I suspect he does."

He looked at me, incredulous. "And you say men are the ones after looks."

"Without money or power, six pack abs are nice consolation prize."

He shook his head. "He's got the abs — and three ex-fiancées. He left each one within a month before the wedding."

I leaned back against the wall next to the kitchen. "Cream of the crop you've got here for me today. Thanks, Brady."

"I kind of forgot about that. Normally, I don't

think about all that bullshit. But with you, I have to."

"Compliment or cut down? I just can't decide."

"You deserve better than that, Jane. Plus, I'm a little scared of you."

I slugged his arm and pushed past him into the bathroom. Truth was, none of his friends would do. Not while he was hanging around. But I had to face the facts — if he was trying to set me up with his buddies, he must not be interested in me. *Deal with it.*

He was waiting for me when I came out. People were clearing away from the table and he dropped a few twenties by the check to pay for our share.

"Thanks," I said.

"I'm lucky I could cover it. I got lousy tips last night because someone was distracting me all night."

My first thought was Miranda, but then I realized he meant me.

"Hey, I could have set you up with Miranda in exchange. She was definitely interested. It's not too late." How much did it suck, saying that?

He looked down at me, and his eyes locked on mine. "I'm not interested."

I sucked in a little breath. "You're going to have to explain that to me one of these days."

He just shook his head. "Maybe one of these days you'll figure it out for yourself."

We stopped walking when we reached my car. "So, day one and no success. I'm still dateless. That T-shirt is going to look so cute on me."

He ignored me. "Good news. My buddy, Dave, is having a barbecue this Wednesday night. Kind of a hump-day thing. How 'bout I pick you up at six?"

"Should I bring anything? Nothing homemade. I'm not that kind of girl." Just wanted to get that out in the open.

"Nope. Just your acerbic wit. I'm sure you'll be serving up rounds of it."

I really didn't want our day together to end. In a movie, this is where we would make an awkward attempt to kiss each other, and it would end up being so awesome, we'd tumble into the car only to emerge rapturous and flushed, hours later. Or maybe interrupted by the police in a slapstick scene.

But he just patted the roof of my car, waiting for me to get in.

So, I climbed in. It was getting late, and duty called at the vet clinic the next day. Poor furry suckers didn't know their early morning joy ride was going to be the end of their manhood. There were three neuters scheduled for the next morning. That's something a girl needed to rest up for.

"See you Wednesday," he said.

I waved goodbye, pretending I wouldn't be counting down the hours. All seventy-two of them.

Brady picked me up in his Wrangler, and I was more excited to see him than the time I saw Santa behind our house the night before

Christmas. I hoped this hot, funny guy wasn't
going to just turn out to be make-believe, too. I
liked him more and more each time I saw him.

"Did you tell Miranda what you're up to?" he
asked.

"Since she lives across the hall from me I
would have, but she's down on the Cape this
week at someone's beach house. Apparently the
dry cleaner is the new place to meet hot men."

"Or at least cleanly dressed men."

"I'm sure he's both. And rich." I was glad I
didn't have to tell Miranda about my "date" with
Brady. She probably would've wanted to come
along and I wasn't willing to share. She had
enough boys to play with.

Brady slowed the car. "Should we make a
detour to the dry cleaner before the party?"

I leaned my head back on the seat and looked
at him. "I'm good, thanks."

"Miranda sounds very different from you."

I snorted. "And you didn't draw that
conclusion the other night from looking at us?"

"No, I mean the way she treats men. Like
an all-inclusive ticket to amuse her. I'm surprised
you're friends with her."

I tightened my grip on my purse. "You don't
understand."

"Of course not, I'm a man. Enlighten me."

I looked out the window, wondering how
much to tell, but still wanting to defend her. "We
met when we were kids. I was nine and she was
eight. We were both in the cancer ward at
Children's Hospital. Leukemia, only hers was
worse. Way worse."

He reached over and squeezed my hand. "I'm so sorry."

His hand on mine was like butter on a biscuit—only I was the one melting. I had to remind myself to keep talking. "Yeah, it sucked. But it sucked more for her. My parents were there all the time. I was never alone. But her mom was single; her dad took off before she was born. Her mom couldn't lose her job, and she could only visit for a little while each day. So, we kind of took her under our wing."

Brady pressed his lips together. "That must have been so hard for her."

I nodded. "And then it got worse. I only had to do one round of chemo. She had to do more. I checked out of the hospital and she was still there." Damn it, tears were pricking my eyes and it was too late to stop them.

"Tissues are in the glove box," he said.

"Thanks." I reached for one and blew my nose, knowing how pretty that must look. "I tried to come back and visit her as often as I could. I felt so guilty, knowing she was there alone. We've been friends ever since. No one else really understands what it's like to go through something like that."

"And you still feel responsible for her?"

I hadn't really ever thought of it that way, but he was right. "Yeah, seventeen years later, I guess I still do." I picked at my thumbnail. "She has a bit of a "live life to its fullest" thing going on, thus her list of conquests. Kids with her type of cancer usually don't live past forty," I said, quietly.

He came to a stop for a red light. "That

explains a lot."

I shrugged. "So don't judge her. And don't judge me for helping her. It seems like fun and games, but it's more than that."

He reached for my shoulder and squeezed it. "You're a great friend, but don't put your life on hold just to make sure she lives hers."

I sucked in a breath. He was wrong. Totally wrong. "I'm not. Not at all. Look at me with you here tonight, trying to wrangle up a date." I swiped a stray tear off my cheek and put my defensive humor back in full protection mode. I hadn't told too many people the story I'd just told Brady. But now it was time to change the topic. "So, who are the lucky fellows today, anyway?"

The car behind us beeped, and he pulled his hand away from me and started driving. "Some friends from college. Good bunch of guys, and they'll love you."

"Where did you go to college?'

"U Mass."

"For their fabulous bartending program?"

"Ouch, that almost hurt. No, I got the most useless degree in the world — political science — and here I am, wondering what to do next."

"Besides counseling dateless women."

"Soon to be formerly dateless women."

"Could be your new calling: matchmaker to the hopeless."

His friend Jack had a fabulous house with a big back yard and a beautiful wife who laid out a spread of food that should've been photographed and put on a magazine cover. I would have been happy dating *her* just for the food. But Brady was right, a few interesting friends were there as well, and he made it clear when he introduced me that I was just his pal.

"Go get 'em champ," he whispered to me. He went into the house, leaving me outside with Brett the dentist, Tony the roofer, and Zach, who owned a store. We wandered over to a horseshoe pit. I was just glad no real horses were involved. That would certainly have had an ugly outcome.

"Jane's on my team," Tony announced. His big, black dog barked his approval and ran over to us.

That made me smile. He was my pick of the bunch, with long, dark hair, a killer tan and muscles to match. And he brought his dog along? I'm in, I thought. I grinned at him. "Confession time, before you tap me for your team."

"Oh, no. You don't play for my team?" He tried to look serious.

I playfully whacked him. "I've never played horseshoes."

"Never to late to learn. Let me show you." He handed me a horseshoe and stood behind me, gripping my hand and showing me how to pull my arm back and throw it toward the pin. I'm certain he could have gotten across the points of the game without the up close and personal demonstration, but that was the most man action I'd had in months.

I threw the first shoe and it clanged against the stake and spun around, dropping to the grass.

He high-fived me. "Holy crap, total natural! Knew I was right about you."

29

I smacked my hand to my forehead. "All these years neglecting this inborn talent. I could've been on my school's horseshoe team."

Brady wandered out with beers for us all and watched, while Tony and I totally creamed the other team. Tony scooped me up and spun me around. "You're awesome." His dog lept and barked, hoping to join the fun. "Even Winston thinks so." He patted his dog's head.

I looked over at Brady, but he wasn't smiling.

Tony sat next to me at dinner, and we had a competition to see who could eat more ribs. He beat me, but only by two. "You eat more than any girl I've ever met."

"Oh, you sweet talker." I nudged him with my elbow. My stomach wasn't rolling like it did at the thought of hooking up with Brady, but I'd be interested in a go round with Tony.

Seemed like he was thinking the same thing. "My uncle owns the roofing company I work for. He's having a picnic for us Saturday afternoon. Wanna come and do some damage in the horseshoe pits?"

I opened my mouth, but Brady answered for me. "Don't you have that charity thing that day? For the sick...cat...society?" He totally faked a cough.

I narrowed my brows, and he fixed me with a stare. "Oh, right. I almost forgot I even signed up for that. How could I have forgotten the Sick Cat Society Gala? Thanks for the reminder. Wouldn't want to let them down."

"Maybe some other time," Tony said, his smile disappearing.

"Don't worry, I've got her number," Brady said.

Which clearly you won't ever give out, I thought.

We said goodnight, and I couldn't wait to confront him in the car. "I forgot, are you coming with me to the Sick Cat Charity Gala?"

He dropped his head back against the seat. "I'm sorry. I couldn't let you go out with him."

"You said these were your nice college buddies. That's why you brought me here, remember?"

"I didn't know Tony was going to be there. He's friends with Jack, but he's not one of my college buddies."

"And what's wrong with him?"

"He's got an arrest record. Drugs."

Shaking my head, I closed my eyes. "Your men just get better and better. But why don't you let me go out with him and decide if he's right for me? People make mistakes. He's even got a job."

"Well, his jeans seem too tight. Doesn't that bother you?"

"They looked good to me. Real good."

He frowned. "I remember being at a party where he was arguing with a woman in the driveway and she left crying."

"Maybe she just found out someone died." I pointed at him. "The point is, making a woman cry doesn't really take him out of the running. Not even the arrest record does. I don't have a man shopping-list like Miranda. My needs are simple. Cute and nice."

"I can't vouch for whether he's nice. I'd have

31

to think jail makes a person not nice. Sorry. I have to say no to this one"

"I'm still dateless. Looks like you're going to be buying me a brand spankin' new shirt."

He ignored me. "I'm not giving up yet. My brother's birthday is this Saturday. I'm taking the night off and you're coming."

"What about the sick cat society? They really need my support." I clasped my hands in a pleading gesture.

He sighed. "Send them a check. I'm afraid you're going to have to cancel and spend the night with me."

I looked out the window and grinned up at the moon.

Miranda came back from the beach a day early. "He started talking about baby names." She lay on my couch and dangled her feet over the armrest.

"At least you can cross beach house off your list."

"True, true." She picked up a Cosmo off my coffee table and started flipping through it. "I'm thinking about working on that bartender from last week. Want to go back there tonight?"

With you? Hell, no.

"He's on vacation this week," I lied. "We'll try another time." I didn't want her anywhere near my crush. He might not be able to help himself. I changed the subject. "How about a sixth-grade sleepover at my place?"

She popped up and headed for the door. "I'll bring the spa goodies."

Miranda came over and we recited every line of *Sixteen Candles* while painting each other's toes. Mr. Mew promptly climbed onto her lap when she settled onto the couch, with a bowl of popcorn tucked between the two of us. Even feline males preferred her company to mine, that traitorous cat. *You think Miranda would shove a pill down your throat when you get worms, you beast? No. She wouldn't.*

Our sleep over would've been the perfect time to tell her the truth about Brady. But I couldn't admit I'd finally fallen for a guy — who was trying to set me up with his buddies. Embarrassing. And I didn't want her pity. It was clear I was just meant to be friends with a guy who I wanted more than a lifetime supply of Godiva. There's no Valentine's Day card for that relationship.

On screen, Jake Ryan kissed Samantha and we both sighed. Then Miranda stretched and shooed my kitty off her lap. "I'm beat," she said. "Off for some beauty sleep."

"Ah, if only that's what it took to look like you."

She bopped me with her pillow. "Shut up, Jane. You're adorable."

"Puppies are adorable."

"Are we going out tomorrow night? There's a new bar downtown."

I wasn't ready for another night fending off her suitors. And I didn't know how long I'd be out with Brady. "I can't. I'm sorry. I've got this sick cat charity event to go to."

She eyed me strangely.

I nodded. "It's for work. Boss'll be mad if I don't go."

"Have fun, if they allow that kind of thing at a sick cat charity event."

"I'm sure I will."

"Has everyone been cleared and vetted ahead of time?" I asked Brady, when he picked me up.

"You never know which stragglers might show up. And we've got a few oddball cousins who could make an appearance, but I think we'll be okay." He gave me a thumbs up.

I smoothed my sundress, and was glad he didn't mention my first appearance in a dress. It was a rare day that I slipped on a dress, but I wanted him to see me as someone more than just funny old Jane.

Thus far, he hadn't seemed to notice.

Plus, we were going to his parents' house and it's always good to make a nice first impression, at least in my world of wishful thinking.

We pulled up in front of a rambling old farmhouse outside the city. The party was in full swing under a big, white tent out back, and as we walked over I could see why Brady had brought me. There was indeed a nice collection of men to choose from. I spotted a Brady look-alike, only a few years younger. "Is that your brother?" I asked, jerking my chin in the direction of the keg.

"Yep. Turning twenty-four today."

"How old are you?"

"Twenty-six."

I gave him a nudge. "Me, too."

"I wouldn't have guessed. You're nowhere

near as mature as me."

I stuck my tongue out at him, and he led me over to meet his brother. "Tad, this is my friend, Jane."

He smiled, and it was almost as dreamy as Brady's. "Nice to meet you. Brady hasn't brought anyone along in a while. Not since —"

Brady cut him off. "We're just friends."

Guess my sundress wasn't that cute after all. I stuck out my hand. "Nice to meet you and happy birthday. One more year till you hit your quarter-century crisis. Ready for it? Now that I'm the ripe old age of twenty-six, I can answer any questions to help ease you through this difficult time."

He took a long swig of his beer and crushed the plastic cup. "I know. Depressing. I figure twenty-five is the year I become an adult. I'll spend the rest of this one partying. Maybe I need the guidance of an older woman to help me through it." His smile almost killed me.

I didn't have a chance to do anything but blush.

Brady grabbed me by the elbow. "Come on, I want you to meet my parents."

"But I was talking to the birthday boy," I protested, as he dragged me away.

He ignored me and waved to a handsome older couple laughing by a big bed of roses. They looked up and smiled. "Brady, darling!" his mother called.

He reached over and kissed his mom and his father patted him on the back. "Mom, Dad, this is my friend Jane."

His mother raised an eyebrow.

"Friend," he emphasized.

He was certainly making that point clear.

"Nice to meet you," I said. "Lovely place."

We chatted a bit, and then a few cousins wrangled Brady away and I found myself talking to Tad again, without my handler.

"So, what's on your birthday list this year, young man?" I asked him, as we walking along the shore of a small pond.

"The usual. Beer, money, a pony." He was a bit shorter than Brady, but he could be a nice stunt double. He seemed just as nice and funny, too.

I tipped my head and raised an eyebrow. "I thought only girls wanted ponies."

"How else can you be a true cowboy without a pony? My parents could never understand that. I thought by asking for a pony instead of a horse, I'd increase my chances, considering how much smaller they are. But no such luck." He shrugged and smiled.

"Sorry to hear it, buckaroo. So, no girlfriend here?" I linked my hands behind my back. "Subtle, right?"

He laughed. "At your age, I'm sure you don't have time to beat around the bush. My mother's hoping this is the year I grow up and find a decent girl, because you know, she was married with a baby at my age."

"Wow, I had no idea mother's played that guilt trip business on their sons."

"Probably because she doesn't have any daughters."

"So, what do you do for a living, irresponsible Tad?"

"I'm a high school gym teacher."

"Oh, those poor girls. "

"It's an all boys school."

"I'm sure you're tormenting a few of them, too."

He laughed, and Brady materialized behind us. We ignored him.

"What do you do?" Tad asked.

"I'm a veterinary assistant."

"And she blew off a very important charity event to be here," Brady said.

I rolled my eyes.

"Hey, I've got a fundraiser for the school next Saturday, a Hawaiian luau to help raise money for new football uniforms. Do you want to come with me?"

"I think I've got a hula skirt kicking around," I said.

"Actually, she's going out with me next Saturday. Remember?"

I looked at him, confused, and before I could say anything, Tad piped up. "Sorry, dude. I thought you two weren't dating."

Someone called Tad's name, and he waved and started walking away. "Talk to you later, Jane."

I glared at Brady and planted my hands on my hips. "Okay, so what's wrong with him—recovering from malaria? Is he a closet cross-dresser?"

"He hates puppies."

"You hate cats, but that doesn't make you a bad guy." I crossed my arms. "Why don't you want me going out with your brother?" Did he think I wasn't good enough for him?

"He's immature and it's bound to end badly. I don't want to get caught in the middle of that. And besides, I am taking you out next Saturday." He led me away from the pond, back to the party tent.

"You're blowing off work again?"

He nodded.

"Haven't we yet mined all your friends and family? Who am I meeting now?"

"No one. We're going out. You and me. For dinner and a movie."

"You're going to pawn me off on the ushers? They're usually high school boys, and last time I checked, that was illegal."

"No. I'm taking you on a date."

"A date?" I narrowed one eye at him. "You're running out of time and you want to win the bet."

He held up his hands. "No, no. I just want to take you out. I'll pick you up at five."

I thought about that long after he dropped me off. If he wanted to take me on a date, why wasn't there any goodnight kiss? Or was he just that desperate to keep me from his brother? Something else was going on here, but I didn't know what.

How in the world do you dress for a date that didn't really feel like a date? I didn't want to get too dressed up, but I didn't want to slum it, either. I had to sneak out for a shopping trip without telling Miranda. The deeper I dug myself, the harder it was going to be telling her about Brady.

But what would I even tell her?

She was having dinner with her mother, so she didn't see Brady pick me up, who was looking kill-me-now hot in a pale blue shirt and dark jeans. Now, if I lived life like Miranda, I would've said screw the date, and come on inside and...

"Hi," I said, pushing those nasty thoughts of my mind. I didn't know what was going on, but I knew the evening wouldn't be ending that way.

Brady was quiet for most of the ride to the restaurant. I joked about his dislike of cats and the collection of bras at the bar being a good resale opportunity on ebay, but it got little more than a chuckle from him.

Once we got to the restaurant and each had a drink, he loosened up a bit. "So, am I allowed to date your brother when he's twenty-five?" I teased.

He looked out the window. "No, I just don't want you to, that's all."

"You didn't have to take me out. You could have said I was leaving for an African photo safari or something."

"I wanted to take you out. Really."

I smoothed the napkin on my lap and looked at him. "You wanted to go out with me on a date." I swallowed hard. "As more than I friend?"

Before he could answer, a tall, blonde woman walked up to our table, and my first instinct had me thinking it was Miranda.

"Brady? How are you?" She set her hands on the table and leaned over, like she was going to pour her cleavage on his plate.

Brady sat up straight. "Laura? I thought you

were in Florida. Did you move back?"

"No, I'm visiting my folks. Who's this?" She jerked her chin in my direction.

"This is Jane. Jane, this is Laura."

"His ex-girlfriend," she filled in.

I gulped and shook her hand. "Nice to meet you." But it wasn't. Not at all. She was tall and thin and gorgeous and reminded me of how I wasn't any of those things. No, Brady wasn't truly interested in taking someone like me out. This was a sympathy date, and that was it. I was like the girl back at the bar who'd scored a free drink. Tall, blonde goddess — that was his type.

"Hope you're doing well," she said. "Nice meeting you, Jane."

He blew out a breath as she walked away. "That was fun," he said.

"When did you two break up?"

"Six months ago. It was kind of ugly. She moved down to Florida and was mad I didn't follow her."

"Do you still love her?"

He snorted. "No. I'm damn glad I didn't follow her there. We weren't right for a number of reasons."

I looked down at the menu, pretending to be enthralled with the description for the chicken Marsala. "She looks a lot like my friend Miranda."

He cocked his head. "I guess she does a bit."

I just nodded and was so grateful I had taught myself how to keep from crying by pinching that space between my thumb and forefinger. My thumb cleavage. It would probably be bruised the next day.

We finished dinner with forced conversation and a few lame attempts at jokes. Afterward, I suggested skipping the movie. "I'm not feeling great," I said.

"Legionnaire's disease, I suspect."

"Probably. Don't even dream of kissing me, I'm probably contagious."

"Fair warning."

We drove home and I had to pinch my thumb cleavage again. This date was such a mistake. He wasn't interested in me, of course not. He just felt bad for me. And how could we keep being friends with this between us now, like a piece of spinach in your teeth that won't ever go away?

I hopped out of the car before any uncomfortable conversation could arise.

"I'll call you tomorrow to make sure you're feeling better."

"Thanks," I said, dashing off to my apartment for a long hot bubble bath and an even longer cry.

After a restless night, I knew I had to talk to Miranda. She'd be mad I didn't tell her about this all along, but she would tell me how to save my friendship with Brady if there was any way to do that.

I heard someone out in the hall and popped up to look through the peephole before I went out. Brady was coming out of Miranda's apartment. I sucked in a breath and flattened my back against the wall. My heart was in my stomach. Miranda hooked up with him, after all. She didn't know how I felt about him, or she never would have.

But of course, I'd been too stupid to tell her about my silly little crush.

I knocked my head against the wall a few times, then jumped back in bed, unwilling to answer the door for him in case he was stopping by my place.

But he never came.

Miranda, however, did. And I wouldn't let her in. Was he after her now? A nice substitute for his ex-girlfriend? Did seeing Laura remind him there was a perfect body double nearby?

I waited for her to stop knocking, quickly got dressed, and left the apartment. I couldn't bear to hear her gushing over the guy I was crazy about. I left a note on my door telling her I was visiting my parents and would be home quite late.

But I didn't feel like crying on Mom's shoulder over this. She'd give me some sickly sweet pep talk about how special I am and how anyone would be lucky to have me blah, blah, barf. Instead, I went to the zoo. I'd probably do too much damage at the mall.

But that didn't cheer me up. It was a miserably hot day, and even the kangaroos just stood there. Not hop in the bunch. Plus, there was no one to share a joke with.

It took everything in me not to answer the phone when Brady called. And he called three times. Miranda did, too. I was hoping in a few days, the idea of the two of them together would be easier to swallow.

But chances were Miranda wouldn't last with him a few days. She ate up her men like they were microwave meals; Brady was a single-serving pizza. And no way would he be settling for me as consolation prize. Hopefully, we could strike up a friendship again in a while, but it would never be like it had been.

I wasn't even going to insist he pay up on his bet and get me that damn shirt.

I managed to avoid Miranda on Monday, too, by heading in to work early and staying late.

She kept calling and finally left a voice mail. "I really, really need to talk to you about Brady."

Delete. Not yet.

I also ignored three more phone calls from Brady. I supposed it wasn't fair. They didn't know I'd seen them together. Miranda would be furious with me for not returning her calls, but I was still hardening up my emotions. Kinda like a crab that had molted and needed to grow its new shell.

Brady's messages were vague. "I really want to talk to you, Jane. Please return my calls. Unless you've got laryngitis. Or donated your vocal chords to science. Please just call."

By Wednesday morning when I dragged myself into work, I was miserable. Even the darling Ragdoll cat we were boarding for a week didn't cheer me up.

I got ready in exam room one for a new client bringing in a kitten. Maybe it would be a cute little bugger who would make me smile. I looked up when the door opened. My mouth dropped, but nothing came out.

"Hi, Jane. I'd like you to meet Fluffy."

"Brady? What are you doing with a kitten?

43

What are you doing here?"

"I needed to see you. You wouldn't answer my calls, you're never home. So, I figured you couldn't refuse a guy with a new cat." He held it up next to his face and smiled.

"Miranda doesn't like cats. Or maybe you two have broken up already? She's like that." God, I could be such a brat.

He set down the cat on the exam table and made a time out sign with his hands. "What are you talking about?"

I looked down and pinched the bridge of my nose. "I saw you leaving her apartment Sunday morning. And Fluffy is such a boring name."

"Why didn't you say something?"

"I didn't know you were getting a cat, or I would have objected."

"No, about seeing me at Miranda's?" His kitten jumped down to the floor, inspecting the place.

"Yes, interrupt your post-coital embrace."

He rubbed his face with his hands while his kitten brushed against my ankles. I picked it up and stroked its head.

"I was over there asking her about *you*."

"Me?" I pressed my hand against my chest. "What about me? If I would object to the two of you getting together?"

"I like you, Jane. I really like you. I didn't realize it at first, but that's why I wouldn't let you go out with any of those other guys. My brother? Only if you want to kill me."

I crossed my arms with the kitty pressed against my chest and tapped my foot. "If you like

44

me, why did you have to talk to her about it?"

His hands circled the air, as he struggled to answer. "For some reason, I can't let you know how I really feel about you without it coming out like a joke. I needed her advice. And no, I'm not interested in someone like her, with her tally of conquests and plans for worldwide man domination. When I met you, it was like I got knocked over the head and could think of nothing but you. Only, getting hit over the head made me too stupid to realize what was going on. I've been a bit gun shy since I broke up with my ex."

He reached for my hand but I gave him his cat instead. This wasn't *Jerry Maguire*. He didn't have me at hello. "But you were acting so strange when we went out to dinner. I definitely wasn't getting any 'I'm interested' signals from you."

He sighed. "I know. I was nervous, and I didn't know how to be serious around you and tell you how I really felt. What if you made a joke out of it?"

I pretended to tidy up the counter, moving a box of plastic gloves around and wiping up a spot that wasn't there. "I thought you were asking me out because you felt sorry for me." Wincing, I thought of the frizzy-haired girl and her chardonnay.

He walked over to me and took me by the arm. "Please, blame it on medication or a mental illness or temporary stupidity. I want you, Jane."

I let the words play back in my head. *He wants me.* "No joke?"

He shook his head. "No joke." He swallowed and looked down at the floor. "I just hope you

45

feel the same."

I turned to him and stared, looking for a trace of sarcasm or teasing. But there was none. I wrapped my arms around him like I'd imagined doing so many times. "I do." I squeezed tightly and pressed my eyes shut. "I've felt this way since the first night I met you."

His hands cupped my shoulders. "I guess I'm a little slow."

"You're worth the wait."

He bent down and brushed his lips against mine. Fluffy jumped onto the exam table and rubbed against my hip, reminding me I was at work. I broke away from our kiss. "I can't do this."

His eyes widened. "What?"

I turned away from him. "I have to examine your cat." I looked at him over my shoulder and smiled. "We'll have to try that again when I'm off the clock."

He let out the breath he'd been holding. "Thank God. I thought you were going to tell me you were joining the Peace Corps."

"Or a nunnery."

"Or worse — starting a list like Miranda's." He came up behind me, wrapped his arms around my waist, and kissed the back of my head.

My stomach rolled in delight. Then I felt guilty for thinking he and Miranda had hooked up. "I need to apologize to her. I haven't returned her calls either."

"You better. Last I checked she was looking at bridesmaid's dresses for what she predicts will be our upcoming nuptials."

I rolled my eyes.

"Well, she *was* checking out venue's for a bachelorette party."

"Now that I believe."

A week later, I wandered into the bar alone, since Miranda was in the Bahamas with her new beau. Still hadn't found an Australian with a yacht, though. But I figure it's good for her to have goals. Brady saw me and waved.

I scowled at the line of girls at the bar. I scanned the rafters for new bras but there weren't any recent additions.

I found a stool and sat down. I tossed a small shopping bag at Brady and he caught it. "What's this?"

"I'm settling up on our bet."

He pulled out the t-shirt and smiled. "I'm taken," he read.

One of the girls in front of him pouted. "Aww, you are?"

He looked at me and smiled. "Yes, I am."

"And his girlfriend is crazy," I told her. "You don't want to mess with her."

"Really?" she asked.

Brady nodded. "She's gotten into fights over me."

"She's been in jail."

"The psych ward," he added.

I nodded. "She even made that shirt just to keep women away."

The girls were wide eyed. "Why are you, like, dating her then?" one asked.

He looked at me and smiled. "She's funny

and beautiful and she gets me."

I held up one finger. "Wait, I thought it was because you were afraid she'd kick your ass if she broke up with you?"

"Well, yes. There's that too."

"Awww, you sweetie," I said, leaning across the bar for a kiss. "But wear the shirt anyway."

His dimples appeared as he smiled and met my lips. "Always."

"Wrong Place, Right Guy"
By Lisa Scott

I was on my way to a bar decorated with bras — wondering if I'd be required to donate mine — when I spotted a cute guy walking toward me. With his sandy brown hair and bright polo shirt, I thought he was potential date material — until he pulled a knife on me.

"Keep quiet, darlin', and we'll be fine." He turned the silver switchblade round and round in his hand as we stood in the empty parking lot.

My heart clobbered my chest and I threw my purse in front of me. "Take it. It's a Coach. It's real." Backing away from him, I clutched the big wallpaper sample book I was returning to the store before hitting the bar. My muscles twitched as if itching to attack. But I was frozen.

He stepped over the purse toward me. "I was interested in the purse until I got a closer look at you." The smell of rank, stale beer hit me. "Guess it's my lucky day."

The knife was inches from my throat. I tried to swallow but my mouth was parched. It was after eight o'clock, and all of the businesses that shared the parking lot were closed. There were a few vehicles, but no sign of anyone. The sun was starting to slip in the sky on the warm summer night, casting long shadows on the pavement.

The man sneered, heat radiating off him. A bead of sweat slid down his tanned face. With his bright white teeth and blue eyes he had looked like a model at first glance. Now he looked like a lunatic.

Such are my dating instincts.

The knife glinted in the sun, as he looked me up and down.

I took another step back. If I had learned anything from my afternoon dates with Oprah, it was never to be taken to the second crime scene. That's where the bad stuff always went down. I had to gather my wits and do something fast.

I held up my hands, trying to invoke the voice of reason. "Just take the purse and no one needs to get hurt. Please."

He laughed. "It won't hurt unless you fight."

I shoved the wallpaper book into his chest, hoping to knock him down, but he grabbed it out of my hands and threw it aside. "Bitch!"

His face was twisted and angry as he lunged for me. When I dodged to the side, a man jumped from the sky, knocking the attacker to the ground with a thud. They scuffled for control, swearing and stirring up dust and dirt. Then the attacker rolled over and held his knife to my hero's throat. "This doesn't involve you."

I should have run, but my adrenaline was MIA. I tried to find my voice to scream for help, but it was gone, too. Apparently, I was born with no survival instincts.

The man on the ground gripped the attacker's arm and head butted him. The bad guy snarled above him and struggled to free his arm — and the knife.

This guy's going to get killed because of me.
That's what finally kicked in my courage. I jumped on the bad guy and straddled him from behind, grabbed his wrist, twisted it behind his back, and wrenched the knife from him.

Just like we'd practiced in Tae Kwon Do class the week before. Without the knife, of course. I stood up and the other man pried his way out from underneath him. I pressed my shiny black pump against the attacker's neck for good measure, the heel poised above his jugular. That wasn't exactly one of our official moves, but he remained pinned to the ground. "It won't hurt unless you fight." But there wasn't much fight left in the guy.

The other man hopped up and ran for my purse. He was shirtless and bleeding.

"What the hell? You're going to rob me now?" I held the knife back like I might throw it at him.

That's when the guy on the ground bit my ankle. I jerked my foot away and he rolled over, taking me down with him, right on my rear.

The other guy dove on him, pushing him away from me.

Pulling myself up into a squat, I pointed the knife at the attacker. "Don't move."

He gazed up my skirt and smiled, blood dripping from his mouth. "Nice panties."

The jumper punched him in the face and the man's head hit the pavement. He didn't move after that, but I kept the knife pointed at him and set my foot on his chest in case he tried to get up again. My heart was ready to burst. I glanced down at my ankle. Luckily, he hadn't broken the skin.

A black dog bounded across the parking lot toward the other guy. "Nice timing, Winston. You show up now?" The dog sat down, his tail thumping the pavement, while the guy went back for my purse. "I'm not stealing it, I'm looking for your cell phone to call police. I don't have mine on me."'

I squeezed my eyes shut, embarrassed. "Sorry, I'm in defense mode." I wiggled my fingers at him. "Bring it here."

He picked up my purse and handed it to me, keeping some distance between us.

I fished out my cell with one hand, dialed 911, and filled the police in on the situation. "I just got held up in the Parkside Shopping Plaza. The attacker's knocked out. Hurry!"

The man rubbed the back of his head and came over to me. "You alright?"

The sound of sirens split the air.

I gulped and nodded, even though I wasn't entirely sure. "Where the hell did you come from, anyway?" I asked. "You just flew in like some kind of superhero." I gestured to the sky.

"Big hero, seeing as how you saved me." He jerked his thumb toward the oil change shop next to us. "I was working late on the roof ripping off the last few shingles, and I saw what was happening." He scratched the dog behind its ear, which set one paw twitching. "And my trusty sidekick here shows up when it's all over," he said to the big black Labrador retriever.

"I'm Kristen Gold, by the way. I'd shake

your hand but I'm holding a knife." I shrugged.

"I'm Tony Malone. And this is my useless dog, Winston. Must have been sleeping in the truck, you beast." He swiped his forehead with the back of his hand. Blood was dribbling from the side of his head into his long dark hair, pulled back with a handkerchief. He had a mustache and goatee, and gleaming tanned skin that covered taut muscles. If I had seen both men approaching me in the parking lot, he's the one I would've been afraid of.

Again, with the infallible instincts.

"I hope they're bringing an ambulance, too," I said. "You look horrible."

He shook his head. "Just a few bumps. I've had worse." He braced his hands above his knees and leaned forward, catching his breath. The man didn't have an ounce of fat on him.

The guy on the pavement was still not moving beneath me. *Is he dead?*

Three cop cars tore into the parking lot. Doors flew open and three officers jumped out, two drawing their guns on the guy underneath me, while another pointed his at Tony.

"Hands in the air, Malone," shouted one of the cops.

Winston growled, while Tony held his hands up.

"He tried to help," I said. "This is the guy you want. The one I'm standing on." I seriously hoped I wasn't breaking any laws. I'd never even gotten a speeding ticket.

The police ordered the guy under me to get up and I stepped away. "This is his knife," I said, holding it out in front of me with two fingers.

The attacker didn't respond, so two officers pulled the man up from the ground. "How the hell did you take this guy down?" one of them asked me. He linked a pair of cuffs on the guy who was now mumbling and incoherent.

I pointed to Tony. "He jumped off the roof and knocked him over. But then the guy pulled the knife on him. So, I disarmed him." I shrugged.

The cop looked me up and down, taking in all five-foot-five of me, and my bulky one hundred and twenty pounds. "How?"

"A few Tae Kwon Do moves, but then the guy bit me, so Tony knocked him out." Didn't need to explain the embarrassing underwear part.

Tony swore. "Why did you wait for me to jump in if you know Tae Kwon Do?"

I pointed the knife at him. "It's a lot different in real life with a crazy man holding a knife than it is when you're practicing on women you invite to jewelry parties." I straightened my skirt and handed the knife to one of the officers.

The short stocky cop took off his sunglasses. "Malone, you got in a fight with this guy?"

He shook his head. "I punched him when he made a rude comment."

"He was trying to save me," I reminded them.

"I should call your parole officer on this."

My mouth dropped. He was a criminal? And now he was getting into trouble because of me?

Tony shrugged. "I finished parole last

month. And it wasn't a fight."

Another cop turned to Tony. "You want us to call an ambulance? Looks like you might need stitches on your head."

Tony waved him off. "Don't bother. I don't have medical insurance, anyways."

I picked up my purse and the wallpaper book and rushed over to him. "I'll pay. You got hurt because of me."

He scrubbed his hands across his face. "How about you just get me a six pack and we call it even? I'm not going to the hospital, and the alcohol will probably help more than anything the doctors will do."

I frowned. "Let me drop off this book and we'll talk this over."

I headed for the paint store, which was my original destination before I was scheduled to join my sister for drinks with the latest guy she was pushing on me. The tiny shopping plaza was off the beaten path, but I'd never considered it dangerous. The ceramic studio where I'd once brought my niece, Lucy, was here, along with an optician's office, the oil change shop and a few empty storefronts. There were a couple of bars a block or two over. That must have been where my attacker had come from.

A police officer caught up to me as I hurried across the plaza. He asked a few more questions as I slipped the book in the drop box. Being the busy body aunt that I was, I'd volunteered to redecorate Lucy's bedroom and the wallpaper sample book was a week overdue.

Knew we should have gone with paint instead.

As we headed back toward Tony and the other cops, the officer stopped me. "Listen, I know that guy helped you out, but you don't want to hang around him."

"Why not?"

"He's got an arrest record, and he's no stranger to fights. Just say your thanks and stay away."

But this news didn't really change my feelings. This guy had lept off a roof to help me and gotten hurt in the process. Who knows if I would have gotten the chance — and the courage — to fight back if he hadn't intervened? But I figured it was best to humor the cop. "Okay, thanks for the heads up."

The officers took our statements and then cleared the scene, while Tony and I stood in the empty parking lot. The day was moments from going dark, and the lights in the parking lot had turned on. "Does it hurt?" My fingers hovered over the gash on his forehead.

He shook his head. "It'll probably hurt tomorrow."

His goatee tickled my arm and I pulled back. "So, you really jumped off that roof?" It was only one story, but still.

"I hung off the side and then pushed off the wall. I didn't realize you were about to kick his ass." He grinned, showing off perfectly straight, white teeth.

Something was off about this guy, but I couldn't put my finger on it. His rough appearance was hiding something beneath. I reached for his arm and brushed off some gravel.

Scratches marked his back and a few tiny stones were stuck in his skin. I set one hand on his shoulder, and used the other to pluck out the little rocks. "They didn't break the skin. Just a few dents." His skin was hot under my fingertips. "Turn around."

He did as I told him without complaint. My fingers grazed his skin, searching for bumps and bruises. My fingers glided over the muscles on his chest and stomach. I sucked in a breath when I saw the backside of his left arm. "You've got a really bad scrape. I think the cop was right—you should go to the hospital. That gash on the side of your forehead looks bad, too." I pulled back and my hands felt warm from the heat of his skin.

He reached up to feel the wound, and then looked at the tips of his fingers, dappled with spots of dark red. "Nah, the blood is tapering off already. I'm fine. You okay?"

I nodded. "If you're not going to let me take you to the hospital, can I at least take you out for a beer? I could use one myself after that." I was feeling a bit shaky now.

He cocked his head. "That cop didn't warn you off?"

Damn it, I was blushing. "I'm a big girl. I can be my own judge of character."

He stared at me. "I have a feeling you're going to pester me until I let you show some sort of thanks."

I nodded. "I am. Smart man."

He laughed. "Not exactly. Let me pack up my stuff and we'll grab a drink."

He loaded some tools in his pickup truck, pulled on a clean shirt, and told me to meet him at a bar on Main Street. "This isn't the best neighborhood for someone like you at night." He opened his door, and his dog jumped in.

I jerked my thumb over my shoulder. "I'm sorry, you didn't see me disarm that guy?"

"You might run into someone with a bigger knife and a worse temper next time. A girl like you can't take any chances."

I raised an eyebrow. "A girl like me?"

Walking closer to me, his gaze swept from my head to my toes. "Beautiful. Rich. Look at how you're dressed."

I shook my head. "I'm not rich." I didn't mention that my parents were. But beautiful? Yeah, I'd take beautiful even if it was just a smoke job.

"It doesn't take much to be considered as rich around here. Don't see too many people looking like you in these parts."

I crossed my arms. "I'm dressed up because I'm going on a blind date." At the bra bar. Impressive, for sure.

"Then you better get to it. Don't worry about me."

I shook my head. "I'm canceling. I'm too upset, and I really want to get a drink. With you."

"Fine. Let's get out of here. I'll meet you at The Sundowner."

He hopped in his old pickup truck with his dog's head hanging out the passenger seat window and made a fast right onto Main Street.

My hands shook as I drove to the bar.

Maybe the cop was right. I didn't know anything about this guy. I didn't even know why he'd been in jail. But still, I needed to thank him. Then I could be on home in my jammies with a bowl or two of ice cream.

I called my sister Beth on the way there. "You're half an hour late," she said. "Rob is just about ready to leave, Krissy."

I hated when she called me that and she knew it. "Some guy just tried to mug me. I'm not coming to meet you guys."

"Oh my god! Are you alright? Do you want me to come over?" This was the perfect mishap that would keep her busy fretting for weeks. She really needed to get a job.

"No, don't come over. I'm fine. Actually, this other guy jumped in to stop him. I'm taking him out for a drink to thank him. Then I'm going home for a long, hot bath. Tell Rob maybe another time." But I was relieved I didn't have to go out with another one of Beth's set-ups. Just because she was bored in her marriage didn't mean she had to play social director for me.

Even if I had been engaged three times at the ripe old age of twenty-six.

"I don't know. Rob's not the kind to be stood up."

"Then maybe Rob's not my type." No maybes about it.

At the pub, I ordered us beer and nachos, but I was far too queasy to eat. Tony quickly polished off the plate. "I skipped my lunch break today," he said, apologetically. He rested his hands on the table. They were streaked with blood and tar. He looked down at them. "Should've washed my hands."

"Me, too." I rubbed my temples. "But I'm too wired up to eat. Nothing like that has ever happened to me before." My butt really hurt from when the attacker pushed me over, but I couldn't exactly rub it.

He tried wiping his hands off on a napkin. "I wouldn't think so. What were you doing there anyway? All those shops were closed."

I looked at the ceiling and rolled my eyes. "Dropping off a way overdue wallpaper sample book. My niece is looking for a new bedroom theme." I lifted a shoulder. "When you're single with no kids, doting on nieces and nephews is a very fulfilling hobby."

He snorted and shook his head. "I was right. Someone like you definitely shouldn't have been in that neighborhood at night."

"What?"

"Nothing. We're just from very different worlds."

I wasn't going to walk down that road. "So, I hope your girlfriend won't mind you being out with me tonight." Surely, someone who looked like him had a girlfriend. No, he wasn't classically handsome, but he was intense, with those dark blue eyes and chiseled features. His hair and goatee made him hot in a dangerous, sexy way. He looked like a man who knew how to take care of a woman, in and out of the bedroom.

Anyone I ever went out with looked like

they had a routine bedtime, a five star safety-rated car, and was sure to pay their credit card balance in advance and in full. None of my exes would've jumped off a building for me, because who knew if insurance covered that?

He shook his head. "No girlfriend right now. Single life suits me fine."

I leaned back against the leather seat of the booth. "Me too. I'm kind of relieved I was able to cancel the date. My sister sets me up with guys she'd be interested in. We have different taste in men."

That earned a raised eyebrow. Then he said, "So aren't you going to ask?"

"What?"

"Why I went to prison. Like I said, I'm fresh off parole."

I took a long swing of beer and thought about getting another. "It doesn't matter what you did in the past. What matters to me is what you did tonight."

He shrugged.

"But maybe you shouldn't have punched the guy. I'd feel horrible if you went back to jail because of me."

He set down his bottle of beer. "He attacked you — and he was looking up your skirt, the perv. You don't deserve that. In the past, like back in college? I might have let that slide. But now I know what kind of people are out there."

I blushed and looked down. No one had ever gotten in a fight over me. I'd never seen a man knocked out on my behalf. "Are you going to be too sore to work tomorrow"?

"Doesn't matter. I'll be there to finish up the roof. I was lucky my uncle took a chance on me when I was released. He's the only one in my family that still talks to me. It's made things difficult for him and some of the other relatives. I can't let him down."

"Well, definitely take several ibuprofen tonight for the swelling and get plenty of rest. Oh, and some ice packs for your head and you might want—"

He reached over, patted my hand and the words disappeared in my throat. Despite the very intimate, stressful encounter we shared, he hadn't touched me. His skin on mine had a surprising effect that made me shiver.

I looked at his hand and then stared into his eyes. Nothing about him made me scared. Nothing about him said, 'Run.'

He smiled. "No need to worry. I plan on downing a few more beers at home and sleeping it off." He pulled his hand away and signaled to the waitress for the bill.

"No, let me get that."

"Ah, right. The obligatory thank you. Fine, you can pick up the check, only because I know it will make you feel better."

It really seemed like a totally inadequate way to thank a man for saving my life.

Then, it was like he was reading my thoughts. "I was in the right place at the right time for once. Usually, I'm in the wrong place at the wrong time with all the wrong people." He grinned. "It was nice for a change"

I jotted down my phone number on the

back of my business card and handed it to him. "Call me if you change your mind about going to the hospital. I can afford it, don't worry."

He took my card and looked at it. "Real estate agent, huh?"

I nodded. "And despite the bad economy, I'm doing fine. Just listed a beautiful Victorian yesterday. I can pay for medical care if you need it."

"Thanks, but I'm sure I'll be fine."

He walked me to my car. "You go straight home and be careful where you go at night from now on."

"I will." I stood there next to my car, inches away from him. It had the nervous feeling of a first date kiss.

He held out his hand. "Nice meeting you, Kristen."

"You, too, Tony. Take care." He stood in the parking lot and watched me drive away.

I couldn't sleep. Whenever I started drifting off, the drunk man's wild eyes appeared before mine and I woke with a start, clutching my quilt. Finally, at three a.m., I cried myself to sleep, letting my mind run in a thousand wild directions with all the horrible things that could've happened. Tony's blue eyes were the last thing I saw before I finally conked out.

"Monica? It's Kristen. I'm not coming in today. I'll get some work done from home."

"Everything okay?" she asked. She served up office gossip like fresh apple pie.

"Just a little run down today. I don't want to get sick." I was too tired and still too shaky to go to work. And I wasn't ready to rehash the story just yet.

But that might have been a bad idea. I tried watching TV and I tried cleaning. But home alone with just my thoughts, I could think of nothing but the attacker—and Tony.

Remembering that he said he'd skipped lunch the day before, I decided to bring him something to eat. It was the least I could do. Beer and nachos seemed like a pretty lame thank you looking back on it the next day.

I drove to the plaza, now filled with cars and customers. Still, my heart sped up and my eyes swept the area for anyone out of place. Four men knelt on the roof of the oil change shop, swinging hammers in the hot sun. I noticed Tony's dark hair brushing his shoulders and smiled. I parked next to his pickup, and Winston's head popped out the side window, tongue lolling off to the side.

"Hi, boy," I said, patting his head. He nudged me with his wet nose.

One of the guys elbowed Tony, who stopped working and looked down at me. I was hoping for a smile from him, but he looked entirely confused.

I heard some good-natured jeering from the other guys as he climbed down the ladder.

"It's a lot easier that way, isn't it?" I teased.

"But not as fast as jumping. Looking for some more bad guys to take down?" He planted his hands on his hips.

"I wanted to see how you were feeling today. And to bring you this." I held up a brown paper bag packed with a tuna sandwich, a banana and a few Oreos. "You said you skipped lunch yesterday."

He wiped his brow with the back of his hand. "I can't believe you remembered that after everything." He took the bag from me. "Thanks. How are you today? I was thinking about you last night."

"You were?" My throat tightened and I set my fingers on my throat.

"I was hoping you had someone to go home to, someone to be with. I think it would've been scary for you to be alone." He fixed his gaze on me.

I shook my head. "No, it was just me. I live alone. And you're right. It was a horrible night. I called in sick today."

He held up the bag. "This is really nice of you."

An older guy climbed down off the roof and walked over. "Tony, take a lunch break. That's an order." He clapped Tony on the back. "He's a good kid. Not surprised what he did for you last night. I knew something was wrong when I saw how slow he was moving today. We forced the story out of him. I was hoping it was something a little more enjoyable though." He winked at Tony and went back to the ladder.

"That was my uncle."

"So you really are hurting today." I reached for his arm and squeezed. "I'm sorry. Why don't we go over to Brookdale Park and sit in the shade?

65

You need a break."

He looked back at the building. "It's better than sitting here in front of these jokers."

"I'll drive."

"Did you notice how sweaty and dirty I am? I'm not fit to ride in a Beamer. Besides, Winston wouldn't allow it. If you don't mind the serious downgrade in transportation, I'll drive." He held open the door for me

An old bedspread covered the front seat, dusted with dog hair. Empty water bottles littered the passenger seat floor, but I squeezed in next to the dog and a big cooler, knowing this was exactly how I wanted to spend my afternoon—in a dirty truck with the ex-convict who saved my life.

We spread his truck blanket on the ground under a tree and Tony cracked open a cooler full of drinks. He finished an entire bottle of iced tea in one long gulp and smacked his lips together. "Never knew manual labor would leave you so thirsty."

There was so much I wanted to ask him about his past, but I didn't want to pry.

"Did you reschedule your blind date?" he asked.

I leaned back against the tree. "No. My sister called this morning and told me the guy was canceling our plans to see Aerosmith this weekend. He thinks I should have come to the bar to meet him anyway. But the good news is she's never setting me up on another blind date." I grinned. It really was good news.

He shook his head and opened another iced tea. "Sounds like you missed out on a winner. Let me guess, is he a lawyer?"

"How did you know? Thing is, I really did want to see Aerosmith."

"Probably saved you from a boring night with him, though."

By this time, I was dying to know what Tony had done to end up in jail. He seemed so nice and polite, so down to earth. But I didn't want to seem like I was judging him by asking, like his answer would determine how I'd treat him.

He propped up one leg and rested his arm on it. "It was drugs."

"What?"

"I wanted to tell you why I went to jail."

Again with the mind reading! "What happened?"

He let out a long breath and looked up at the cloudless sky. "I was in college. Cornell, pre-law. I was headed right in the direction of your date last night, I'm sure."

"Did you fall in with the wrong crowd?"

He laughed and shook his head. "No, I just fell. During a lacrosse game and broke my thigh when another guy landed on top of me. That's one of the most painful bones you can break. Got hooked on the Oxycodone they gave me for pain. My family doctor is my Dad's friend, so he didn't have any problem writing my new prescriptions when I lost my new bottle of pills, or accidentally knocked them down the sink, or when they were stolen. I had a thousand excuses for new prescriptions. My friends wanted them, too. So, I started selling them." He closed his eyes and shook his head. "I was so stupid."

I reached over and rubbed his arm. "You were young. Stupidity is a side effect."

He looked at my hand and I pulled it away. "How did you get caught?"

"Sold to an undercover officer at school. It was in the newspaper. My parents were humiliated. My father's a lawyer here in town and was disgraced. They wouldn't even bail me out before the trial. Haven't talked to me since." He closed his eyes.

"I'm sorry."

He sighed. "Don't be. It was my own damn fault. But I'm trying to get my shit together now."

"Have you thought about going back to college?"

"With what money?" He shook his head. "No, I'm too old and roofing suits me fine. I don't mind being out in the fresh air on top of a roof after spending a few years under one. My life's on a different path now."

I reached for a drink from the cooler and sat closer to him. "You're not the only person to ever disappoint their parents. Mine have pretty much given up on marrying me off. I've broken off three engagements very close to the wedding. Cost my father thousands. He says if I ever do get married, I'm paying for it myself." I shrugged.

"Do you think you ever will?"

I looked down, embarrassed by my admission. "Not for a long time."

He propped his hands on his knees and swung the empty bottle between his legs. "So, what's the deal with that?"

Our conversation was becoming much more personal than I had imagined. More like a fourth date than a first. *This isn't a date.* I plucked a tiny daisy from the grass and twirled it in my fingers. "I guess I'm afraid of making a mistake." I looked up at him. "What if I pick the wrong guy?"

"Then you start over again. Sometimes you have no choice."

We were quiet for a while, watching kids zoom down the slide at the other end of the park. With a tentative finger, I traced the tattoo of a chain on his shoulder. "Did you get this in prison?"

He looked over at it. "No, when I got out. As a reminder not to screw up again."

"Are you staying out of trouble? The cop said you've been in fights."

He nodded. "I've got some stupid friends who get themselves in bad situations."

"Maybe you need to find new friends."

"Not everyone can overlook a person's past. You probably think differently of me now. And forget trying to get a date. Once a woman finds out, she's not interested." He frowned. "Or her friends interfere to protect her."

I shook my head. "You're a nice guy who made some bad decisions. I think if you hadn't broken your leg, you'd be practicing in a law firm right now." I pointed my daisy at him. "A bad decision doesn't make you a bad guy."

"You're more open minded than most." He packed up the trash from lunch. "And my uncle will only put up with so much, so I've gotta get back to work." He stood up and offered his hand to pull me up.

I took his hand, and when I stood up we were closer than I realized. I looked up at him and my mouth was inches from his. I smiled. "This was nice."

He was still holding my hand, but his fingers slipped from mine and he stepped back. "Nicer than I deserve."

I was finishing up a property search for a client later that night, when I was surprised by a phone call from Tony. Had he changed his mind about going to the doctor?

"Still want to go to the Aerosmith concert?"

I turned off my computer. "Not with the lawyer."

"I've got a buddy who works at the arena. He hooked me up so I could buy a pair of tickets."

I gripped the phone. "I'd love to go."

"I'll pick you up tomorrow at five."

And that left me a long time to wonder, *What's this all about?* He certainly didn't owe me any thanks. But my heart pitter-pattered at the thought of seeing him again.

With fresh clothes and a shower, Tony was even hotter than the first time I saw him. I could easily imagine him in a suit, with close-cropped hair and a cleanly shaven face, arguing a case in front of a jury. The long hair and goatee was probably a nice disguise to keep him from seeing what he could have been. But I liked the Tony standing in front of me with a bottle of wine.

"We've got time for a drink before we have to leave." He stood in the hallway, looking me over.

I wanted to break the silence, but couldn't find the right words; I was too entranced by his gaze, wondering what he saw. I smoothed my hands over the skinny jeans hugging my hips and tried to steady myself on my high-heeled sandals.

Finally, he stepped forward and handed me the wine. "You look great, Kristen."

"Thanks."

I walked to the kitchen and pulled out two wine glasses and an opener, exposing my tummy as I reached. I felt him watching me, and wondered what his rough hands would feel like on the soft skin of my belly. I looked over and our eyes locked.

I quickly looked away. "Let's go outside." I led him to the deck off my family room.

"Nice place," he said.

He sat next to me at the picnic table, and our legs brushed up against each other. I didn't move mine; neither did he. I liked the feel of him against me. "I've had the inside scoop on some great deals. Just bought this last year. Do you have a house?" I asked the question before I realized my mistake.

He shook his head with a soft laugh. "No, I live in a crappy apartment across town. And I was lucky to find it. Not many landlords are willing to rent when you've got an arrest record." He pulled the cork out of the bottle and poured us each a drink. "But I'll have my own place some day."

I took a swallow and willed myself not to say anything else stupid for the rest of the night. "This is good."

He swirled the wine in his glass. "I had a girlfriend back in college who was into wine. She thought I was the one and wanted to be sure I was cultured enough for her standards."

"Nice."

"Thing is, it didn't even bother me. I wanted to be like that for her."

"Whatever happened?"

"She broke up with me when I got arrested."

"Sounds about right. At least she gave you an education in wine." I smiled at him over my glass.

"So, why did you end up breaking things off with your fiancés?"

I set down my glass and stared out over my lawn. The roses crawling up the arbor in back were just starting to bloom. "I was more in love with the idea of getting married than getting married to them." I shrugged. "It's hard to explain. I just knew it wasn't right. Actually, I think I knew that when each one of them proposed, but it was hard to say no. I wanted to believe it could work out. That's what everyone expected me to be doing. Getting married." I shook my head, my long crystal earrings grazing my face. "I was young and dumb."

He spun the wine glass round by its stem. "I think you were smart, not getting into a situation that wasn't right for you."

I pressed my eyes shut. My voice came out in a strangled whisper. "You have no idea how embarrassing it is to have three broken engagements to your name."

He ran his finger down my arm and I shivered. "Probably no worse than an arrest record," he said.

I nodded, feeling like a jerk complaining about the love landmines from my past. It was nothing compared with what he'd been through. "We should probably go."

We headed for the driveway and he opened the door of his truck for me. "Winston must have been mad he couldn't come," I said.

"You have no idea. I expect my couch will be torn up when I get home."

We had great seats at the concert, and I hated thinking about how much he spent on the tickets. I had no idea how much a roofer made, but it probably wasn't much. Once Aerosmith hit the stage, the teenaged girls seated next to me were up and dancing, bumping into me, so Tony pulled me in front of him and set his hands on my shoulders.

His hands were big and warm. I could feel the hard, smooth calluses on his palms against my skin. If his fingers traveled up my neck, they'd feel how fast my pulse had quickened. He was a head taller than me, and I leaned back against him, fitting nicely in his arms.

Despite the thousands of people in the arena and the deafening music, I could only concentrate on the intimate details between the two of us: the way his hands slid down and looped around my waist; how he rested his chin on my head; the way my lips tingled and burned as I thought about kissing him.

I turned my head and looked up at him. I tried to smile, but I could only part my lips. His pupils widened and he bent down and dragged his lips over mine, turning my shoulders so I was facing him. He ran his thumb along my jaw line and then pressed my chin, opening my mouth wider.

I wrapped my arms around his neck. "That's better," I said, taking his mouth in mine.

He pulled me against him and snaked one hand through my hair.

"Get a room," someone behind us hollered.

I tipped my mouth to his ear. "That's not a bad idea."

A grin split his face. "Wanna get out of here?"

My throat was too thick to let the words out, so I just nodded.

He took my shaking hand and led me down the row, up the stairs and out of the arena. We ran through the parking lot. "Where to?" he asked, as we approached his truck.

"My place. It's close enough."

We reached his pickup and he pinned me against the side, taking my face in his hands, then swiping his lips across mine with a teasing lick before unlocking my door.

His grin was wicked. "Well, hurry up then." He helped me in.

He pushed his speed only eight miles over the limit. "Straight as an arrow these days."

I squeezed his hand, realizing what he had risked by punching that guy.

He flicked on the radio, but it didn't ease the

tension between us — two people who knew what they were getting into, with time to talk themselves out of it. But there was no question — I wanted Tony.

We were at my house before I knew it. I dashed to the front step, Tony's fingers wrapped around mine. He rested his hands on my hips as I tried to unlock the door. I dropped my keys, and then fumbled to get the door open.

We tumbled inside, and his arms were around me again, pushing me back until I was against a wall. He braced his hands behind me. "Are you sure about this?" His chest quickly rose and fell, brushing mine.

I looked up and gave him a brisk nod. "And don't make me take you down. You know I can."

He lifted the hair off my cheek and curled it around his finger. "Hell right. Incredible turn on." He gently tugged my hair, pulling my face to his.

I kissed him again, wrapping one leg around his, realizing I better get him to my bedroom, because things were moving more quickly than I imagined. I led him down the hall with no idea where this whole thing was headed — besides my bed.

I woke the next morning with a smile and sore limbs. Then I opened my eyes and frowned. Tony wasn't in my bed. I scrambled out from under the covers and pulled back my curtain. His truck was gone. My heart dropped. After hours of wordless, incredible passion, I'd spent the night in his arms, talking about everything from my first kiss to my favorite foods.

I pulled on my robe. I knew we were different in many ways, but when I was with him, it just didn't seem to matter. In bed in the dark, with his arms looped around my waist, none of it seemed to matter. Our night together had been amazing and I wanted more.

But maybe it'd been enough for him.

I sighed and wandered into the kitchen to make coffee, when the front door opened. Tony held up a box of donuts and a travel tray with two coffees. "Powdered jelly, right? I wasn't sure how you took your coffee, so I got black. Forgot to ask you that last night. I parked on the road, so I wouldn't block you in."

I ran to him and he set down the food and drinks. I grabbed his arms and looked up at him. "I thought you left," I whispered in a voice that sounded more scared and hurt than I intended.

"Hey." He kissed my head. "I'm sorry. I thought I could sneak out and surprise you, and I had to let Winston out." He wrapped his arms around me and squeezed. "I'm not leaving until you tell me to."

I nodded and pointed to the food. "Bring that to bed."

He followed me to my room with the coffee and donuts. I dropped my robe and sat on the bed, patting the spot next to me.

Tony set the coffee and donuts on my nightstand and pulled off his shirt. In a flash, he was back in bed with me. He broke a powdered donut ring in half and held it out. I took a bite, and he popped the rest in his mouth.

I gestured to his lips. "You've got a little powder there." Reaching over to brush the white dusting off his lips, he grabbed my hand mid air and kissed my fingertips, while licking off the sugary residue.

"Never thought I'd find something I like more than donuts and coffee first thing in the morning." His lips made their way down to my mouth, where he paused to lick my lips, goosing a round of shivers in me. He noticed and grinned. "But being here with you like this blows coffee and donuts out of the water." He laced one hand around the back of my head and drew my mouth to his.

I returned his sweet, sugary kiss, thrilled that the passion we'd shared the night before had meant something to him, too. I glanced at my alarm clock displaying the time: nine-ten a.m. I couldn't hold back my smile. "Morning lasts another three hours if you like it that much."

After enjoying him, then the rest of the donuts and coffee, we tried to get dressed, making plans to catch an afternoon movie. But we only got as far as underwear and the couch in my family room. "Forget the movie," I told him between kisses. "I have plenty of DVD's right here."

He rolled me over on top of him and somehow, I didn't hear the front door open.

"Kristen? Come out and stop sulking. It was just a hold-up. Mom and I are here with..." My sister stopped walking when she got into the family room. She dropped a bakery bag. "Oh, my god," she whispered.

I sat up and fumbled for the blanket draped over the back of the couch. But not before my mother walked in the room, holding a plate of cookies.

"Darling, where are you?" Her eyes widened and her hand flew to her mouth. "Oh, my. Oh, my word." She turned around in a circle, unsure where to go or where to look.

I wrapped the blanket around myself and stood up. I pulled Tony up from the couch in his boxers. "This is Tony. From the parking lot the other day."

My mother's gaze went from the dragon tattoo on his calf to the six-pack abs and bare chest, to his goatee and long hair. "You brought home your attacker?"

I dropped my head back and groaned. "This is the guy who saved me." The blanket started slipping and I pulled it back in place.

Tony stepped forward and held out his hand. "Nice to meet you, Mrs. Gold."

She gave him a weak smile and didn't take his hand. "You too," she whispered. She yanked her sweater closed in front of her. "Thank you for helping our Kristen." She stared at the floor.

Beth's eyes bulged. "Can I talk to you? Privately?"

"I'm going to go get dressed," Tony said, heading for the bedroom.

"Good idea," my mother said. She looked at her cookies, neatly stacked on a new silver-serving platter under pink cellophane wrap. "I'll take these into the kitchen."

With the blanket still wrapped around me,

Kristen dragged me into the bathroom. "What are you doing? Are you crazy?"

I yanked my arm out of her grasp. "What?"

"What are you doing hooking up with someone like him?" She shook her head. "You should not have blown off Rob. He is a catch and a half and you're lucky he agreed to go out with you after..."

"Three broken engagements?" I pulled a robe off the back of the bathroom door and slipped it on.

She shrugged. "Word gets around, sis."

I tied the robe belt in a tight knot. "I like Tony. And I'm in charge of my love life. Keep your promises and don't fix me up with anyone else."

"But you'll take him out there? He looks like a criminal."

"You know what? He was. But he's turning his life around and looks like I'm going to be part of it." I surprised myself by saying that. But now that I'd been with him, I didn't see myself leaving anytime soon. "You might as well get used to it now."

She set her hand on my arm and softened her voice. "I think you're just a little confused after what happened. You probably just think you owe him something."

I stepped back from her and knocked my moisturizer off the sink. "I think you and Mom better go. If you hadn't noticed, I've got company. And next time use the doorbell, or better yet, call first."

I went back to the family room and Tony came out of the bedroom wearing his jeans and shirt from the night before. "I should get going so you all can visit."

I grabbed him by the arm. "Actually, they were just leaving. We've got plans today."

He arched an eyebrow.

My mother and sister made a quick path for the front door. "Call me later!" Mom said.

I closed the door behind them, and leaned back against it.

"That was fun." Tony joined me against the door and wrapped his arm around my shoulders.

"I'm sorry about that. The key was supposed to be for emergencies. I guess they thought not hearing from me since the hold-up was an emergency." I shrugged.

"Hey, they care. Not everyone has that, you know."

"They care as long as I do what they want me to."

He stepped away. "And I take it, they don't want you with someone like me."

I twisted my lips. "They were surprised, that's all. And I don't care what they think. Dating their type has only gotten me three broken engagements."

He took my hands in his and raised them over my head against the door. He nudged his nose against mine. "So, what are these plans you promised?"

"You're going to have to get undressed again to find out."

Finally, by dinnertime we decided we needed to go out for food. "Let me take a shower first."

"I'll join you," he said.

I pushed him out of the bathroom. "We'll never get out of here if that happens. We'll take turns."

I tried my best to get ready quickly, but it takes a while to blow out my hair. By the time I was dressed, made up and ready to go, I found Tony on the couch, freshly showered. And asleep.

I leaned over and kissed him. "Wake up, sleeping beauty. I'm ready."

He jumped up. "Sorry. What time is it?" He squinted at the clock. "Wow, it took an hour to get ready?"

I swept my hand in front of me. "You think this just happens naturally?"

He pulled me to him. "You looked pretty good to me this morning. I want to take you to this restaurant my buddy's brother just opened up. A greasy spoon, but it's good, and I want to support him."

I grabbed his hand and squeezed it. "That sounds great."

I couldn't finish the gigantic burger I'd ordered or even half the fries. "This gets five stars from me. Good stuff." I shifted on the stool at the counter wondering if I'd be able to drag myself to his truck.

A group of people came in the front door and Tony turned to look. He raised his hand to greet them. "Hey, Jason. Haven't seen you in a while."

I swiveled around on my stool. Two guys in black leather jackets walked in with three women, also wearing leather and jeans. I started counting

the face-piercings between the five of them, but
stopped. I'd been too chicken to get my ears
pierced until I was sixteen. I couldn't imagine one
in my nose.

They walked over to us and I held my breath.
The women were checking out my strappy
sandals and sundress that really were too fancy
for the place. I smoothed my hand down the silky
material on my thighs and forced a smile. "Hi," I
said.

"Who's this?" Jason asked.

Tony put his arm around me. "This is Kristen.
We met the other day. Kristen, these are some
friends I know from Mackie's bar."

"Nice to meet you," I said, toying with a lock
of my hair, although none of them offered their
names.

The women's eyes flicked back and forth
between the two of us. "And where did the two of
you meet?" one of them asked, incredulously.
"Did you fall through her roof?"

Tony laughed. "It's a long story."

"He saved me from a guy trying to steal my
purse." I set my hands on my knees and
shrugged.

Their eyes wandered to my purse, sitting on
the counter, probably trying to size up whether or
not it was real.

"I think he had more than that in mind."

I squeezed his bicep. "Tony jumped off a roof
and tackled him."

"Yeah, but you pulled the knife away." We
were smiling at each other, and I realized we
probably looked like one of those couples you'd

like to smack.

He kissed my cheek and I noticed one of the women rolling her eyes. Another one snapped her gum and spoke up. "I suppose this means I should tell Sheila you ain't interested." She looked up at the clock on the wall. "She gets done at the plant in half an hour and was going to meet us here. If you don't want to see a grown woman cry, you should probably take Barbie here and go."

I stiffened, and Tony squeezed my shoulder. "Jessie, I'm just not interested in Sheila, I'm sorry. She's a great girl, but not for me."

The woman looked me over again. "I see."

"Don't worry, we were just leaving." Tony tossed some money on top of the check and stood up. He reached for my hand and helped me off the stool.

"Nice meeting you all." But it wasn't. I knew they were making assumptions about me based on my clothes and the way I looked.

"Sorry," Tony said, when we got into his truck. "I think they were a little intimidated by you."

I blew my bangs off my forehead. "Guess we won't be double dating with any of them. We won't be doing dinner with my family or yours, and your friends won't be inviting us out any time soon."

"There really doesn't seem to be a place for us."

"Besides bed," I joked. But he didn't laugh.

He pulled out of the parking lot and looked out the window. "I'm gonna get you home. I don't usually go on forty-five hour long dates. Winston won't talk to me for a week."

"Has it been forty-five hours?"

"I've been keeping track."

I pouted. "I wish you'd stay over again."

"Any longer than two days, and Winston becomes part of the deal."

"That wouldn't be a problem."

He looked over at me for a long moment as we drove along. "Kristen, I had an amazing weekend with you. But I am what I am. That's not going to change. A few days with me might be amusing, but I'm not long-term material. Won't be for a long time."

"What are you talking about?"

He slammed one hand on the steering wheel. "I can't offer you anything."

I sighed. "Would you stop listening to whatever crap your parents told you? You aren't your criminal record. You're Tony. A funny, kind and brave guy. And I really, really like you." I wouldn't be able to explain how I knew that so soon, but I knew. I felt safe with him. And not just safe from bad guys lurking in the shadows, but safe to be myself.

He shook his head. "I can't take care of you."

I pressed my hand against my chest. "I don't need someone to take care of me. I want just someone to care about me, and not consider how I'm going to look on their life resume, or propped up in their fancy home."

"I'm sorry."

"I don't want you to leave. Please. Let's stop

and get Winston and bring him home." I pressed my eyes shut, afraid I'd see him shaking his head no.

He pulled into my driveway and got out to open my door. He hugged me and kissed my head. "This was a great weekend, but it's time to go back to the real world. And in that world? We don't belong together."

I crossed my arms and swallowed back a sob. "Were you just using me?" But the words sounded stupid coming out of my mouth. I knew I had meant to something to him. But he couldn't get over his past. And that wasn't something I could change.

He walked me to my door and squeezed my hand. The he stepped out into the night. I said nothing. I refused to say goodbye.

Tony didn't call. Two days passed and I drove by the shopping plaza, but they had finished the roof and moved on to another job.

Just like he'd moved on from me.

I parked in the lot and cried. We had such a fast, strong connection, but he couldn't get beyond his past. For once I knew—knew in my heart was in love—and I couldn't have him. Was I cursed? I get the ones I don't want, but can't have the one man I do?

My mother and sister called and tried to sound sympathetic over news of the crash-and-burn relationship, but I'm sure they were thrilled I wasn't with him anymore. An ex-convict in the family would be about as welcome as a tick on one of Mom's prize-winning Yorkies.

"Honey, you need to get out and have some fun," my mother said over the phone. "Daddy's company gets tickets for the Children's Hospital Charity Ball every year, but he can't make it this time. Come with me. We'll go shopping and get you a new dress. Then we'll get our hair and nails done. It'll be a hoot."

I didn't answer.

"Please? I really need to go for your father, and I won't go alone."

She knew she had me. I rarely disappointed my father. "Fine. We'll go."

We went shopping and I let her pick out my dress. She surprised me by choosing a lovely cream cocktail dress for me that fit like it was made for me.

"Hey, after three wedding gowns, I know what looks good on you."

I pretended to be hurt, but it was the first time she'd joked about my string of engagements.

Work was slow the next few days, and I only had few houses to show. The Victorian was turning out to be a tough sell, despite how gorgeous it was. It was an estate and the house needed some work, but the family wasn't ready to make any changes. With business slow, I had plenty of time to work on Lucy's bedroom. She'd changed her mind from a seashore theme to a Fairy Princess Kingdom after going on a *Tangled* binge, watching the movie two times a day for a week. We'd decided to try painting a mural.

"Aunt Kristen, Rapunzel isn't smiling! None of your people are smiling." Lucy sat down on the floor with a humph.

I looked at the figures I'd drawn and she was right. I just couldn't conjure up the enthusiasm for a happily-ever-after. "I'm sorry. I'll erase them and start over."

"I've got a better idea." Her eyes widened and she smiled. "Can we do a kitty room instead?"

I laughed. "I've got nothing else to do. Why not?"

That Saturday, Mom and I arrived at the event primped and polished. I caught a glimpse of myself in the mirror of the hotel ballroom and wished Tony could see me looking like this. But that would probably just make him feel more distant from me.

Mom and I each took a flute of champagne from a passing waiter. My mother wanted to mingle, but I just wanted to find my seat. She frowned at me. "Party pooper."

I went to our table and picked up one of the programs, leafing through it to keep me occupied. It was going to be a long night, filled with vapid conversation from the kind of people I couldn't stand — people who cared more about appearances and status than the true value of a person.

I scanned the ads from the evening's sponsors and my eyes froze on a listing for Malone, Mancuso and Fiore, Attorneys at Law. Malone. Tony's father was a lawyer. It had to be him.

I went back to the registration table. "Hi, can you tell me which table the Malone law firm is at? They're friends of the family."

The lady scanned the list and her finger stopped mid-list. "They're at table eleven."

"Thanks."

I headed for their table, not sure what I was going to say. Several people were gathered nearby, and I had no idea who his parents were. I walked up to a man with eyes just as blue as Tony's and he stopped talking. "Can I help you?"

"Are you Mr. Malone?"

"Yes."

My heart sped up, almost like it had when the attacker first showed me the knife. I took a deep breath. "My name is Kristen Gold. I'm a friend of your son's."

"Are you related to Dick Gold, of Gold Insurance Partners?"

"Yes, that's my father."

He held out his hand. "Pleased to meet you. I didn't know you were friends with my son, Nick."

"I'm not. I'm friends with Tony."

His smile disappeared and his wife wandered up to us. "What is it, dear?"

"She knows Tony."

She pressed her lips together.

I squared my shoulders. "That's right. But you don't know him. Not anymore. He saved my life last month."

His mother looked up. "What?" She pressed her hand against the string of pearls around her neck.

I nodded. "I was held up at knifepoint in a parking lot where Tony was working. He jumped off the roof and knocked the guy away from me. I don't know what would have happened to me if he hadn't been there. He's a good person. I got to know him...really well." My voice quavered.

His father set down his drink and crossed his arms.

"I really care about him. But he's convinced he's a rotten person who doesn't deserve 'someone like me.'" I made air quotes around the last part. "And maybe if he had the support of his family as he tries to turn his life around, he'd have a different opinion of himself." My voice was getting louder and a few people had turned to look.

"You do know about his past, don't you?" his father asked. His face was reddening, but I didn't care.

"Yes. He told me everything. Haven't you ever made a mistake?"

"No one in our family has ever been incarcerated." He hissed the last word.

"Has anyone in your family ever saved a stranger? He deserves a second chance. And you deserve to have someone like him in your life. He's a good man." I looked around the room. "Do you know why we're here tonight? To help sick children. Children who might die. But yours is alive and you've cut him out of your life." I shook my head, disgusted. "It's not too late to patch things up. You both deserve it."

His mother set her hand on my arm. "You're absolutely right, dear. And maybe you should tell this all to Tony."

I looked down at my gold shoes. "He doesn't want to see me. He thinks he has nothing to offer me."

"He's here tonight."

I stepped back. "What?"

She nodded. "With his uncle. His roofing company sponsored a table. We were quite surprised to see him. He hasn't come over to us yet." She wrung her hands. "I do hope he does." She looked at her husband. "Don't we, dear?"

Mr. Malone was gripping the chair in front of him and said nothing.

I spun around, searching the room for Tony. His mother took me by the arm and pointed to the far corner. "He's over there." She squeezed me arm. "Thank you," she mouthed.

I smiled at her and sucked in a breath. I headed across the room, wondering what he'd think when he learned I'd confronted his parents. His back was to me, but I knew it was him with his dark hair pulled back in a neat ponytail. His uncle saw me first, and tried to suppress a smile, but Tony turned around to see who he was looking at.

I couldn't keep back my own grin. "What are you doing here?" I touched his face. "You shaved? You look incredible."

He cheeks turned pink and he looked down at his feet.

His uncle clapped him on the back. "Tony here is looking to get into management. Has some great ideas about expanding the company, managing some of the work sites. He's been moping around lately, so I dragged him here tonight."

Tony jabbed his uncle with his elbow.

"I'll leave you two alone." His uncle

wandered away.

"What's this all about?" I asked. "It sounds really great."

He set down his drink and took me by the arms. "You made me want more for more life. I was miserable without you. I figured I needed to make some changes fast so I could prove to you I deserved you."

I shook my head. "You didn't have to prove that to me."

"Fine, I had to prove it to myself."

I hugged him. "You'll always be able to keep a roof over our heads."

He laughed and lifted me off the ground.

"Do you know your parents are here?"

He nodded. "I've been working up the courage to talk to them."

I bit my lip. "I might have said a few things to them."

His eyebrows shot up. "Like what?"

"That you're wonderful and they're ridiculous for not giving you a second chance. I think your mother's on board."

He sighed. "It was my father's idea to cut me out."

"Let's go talk to them." I linked my fingers in his.

He squeezed hard. "You want to?"

"I want them to see what I see in you. And I'll slap them if they don't."

"Better than one of your Tae Kwon Do moves."

I laughed, and we walked over, holding hands. My mother caught sight of us and hurried over. "Honey, who is this?"

I stopped and looked up at the ceiling. "It's Tony. You met him at my house that morning you barged in?"

Her mouth turned into a tiny 'o.' "You clean up nicely." Her eyes swept over him.

"I'll catch up with you later, Mom. We're going to talk to his parents."

"We're not paying for another wedding, Kristen, if that's what this is about," she called behind me.

I heard Tony chuckling and I pulled him along. "You thought I was kidding, didn't you?"

"You can't pick your parents."

"Unfortunately."

I felt him take a deep breath as we approached his parents' table. His grip on my hand tightened. Several people stopped talking as we approached.

His mother ran to him, and set her hand on his cheek. "Oh, Tony." She pressed her cheek against his chest and started to cry. She looked at me and reached for my hand. "We met this lovely friend of yours. Is this your girlfriend?" She looked up at him and he looked at me.

I nodded.

"Oh, Tony." She started crying again and he rubbed her back.

"It's going to be okay, Mom. Everything is working out."

His father stepped forward. "It's good to see you, son. Sounds like you're doing well."

Tony nodded. "I am. I am now."

His father offered his hand. "I thought we'd

lost you." Tony gripped his hand, and his father placed his other hand on top.

I restrained myself from shouting that he had abandoned Tony, not lost him, but things were working out well, so I kept my mouth shut.

"Why don't you two join us for dinner?" Mr. Malone asked.

"Oh, I'm sitting at table twenty-two with my mother."

Mr. Malone turned to two couples that were sitting at the table and pretending they weren't listening. "Tim, Jordan, you don't mind swapping seats with these folks, do you?"

The two men quickly scooped up their dates and transferred to our table, and Tony and his uncle made his way over, too.

We endured the retelling of toddler tantrums and childhood mischief. No secrets were left untold by the end of the night.

"We've already footed the bill for three cancelled weddings, but I think we might be able to swing one more. I have a feeling this one is going to stick," my mother said with a wink.

Then she and Tony's mother were off, talking about reception venues and florists. I didn't dare interrupt. I just looked at Tony and smiled. Then I leaned over to him and whispered, "Meet me at my place later. And bring Winston."

"Ah, you're just afraid to be alone at night now."

I whacked his arm.

"You know, if I do that, I might never leave," he said in a serious tone.

I nudged his nose with mine. "Good. Because

I won't ever let you leave again."

He reached for my hand and kissed it. "I didn't think guys got fairy tale endings, too."

"The good guys always do." I smiled at him and looked in his eyes. Instead of the pain of his past, I now saw the promise of a bright and happy future.

"Not You"
By Lisa Scott

Carly snatched her fourth champagne from the passing waiter and downed it in one gulp. Licking her lips, she set the flute on an empty table.

Her friend Tara placed a hand on her shoulder. "Slow down. We're at a charity event for Children's Hospital. There's no bouncer to carry you out of here."

"That only happened once." Carly held up a pink-tipped finger. "And I promise not to give away my bra this time." She hiccupped. "I'm not wearing one." She'd never been able to walk into McGinty's after that.

She sank down into the nearest seat, not even at her own table. "How else am I going to get through the night? I'm going to my mother's third wedding tomorrow and I haven't even had one of my own. Can you say spinster?"

"Spinster." Tara adjusted her sparkly wrap and sat next to her. "That's a stupid word, anyway. Single old ladies don't spin anything anymore."

Carly groaned and settled her chin in her hand. "Somebody implanted me with a tracking device to find the absolute worse guys. But my Mom was born with a lucky horseshoe up her—"

"That's not true. And it'll all be over tomorrow."

Carly sniffed. "Maybe if I had a date to bring with me it would be easier."

"Plenty of eligible bachelors here tonight."

She swept her arm like she was showing off the prizes on a game show.

Carly scanned the ballroom for some prospects and noticed a tall guy with gorgeous dark hair pulled back in a ponytail—who had just scooped up a blonde woman in his arms like he was never going to let her go. *Typical. I spot a hot guy and he's taken.* "I've just got incredibly bad boy Karma."

A couple wandered over to the table. "I think you've got the wrong seats," said a prissy brunette.

Tara pulled Carly up by the hand. "Come on, let's go."

Bored with the prime rib and political debate being served up at the table, Carly excused herself to get some fresh air on the outdoor terrace. She grabbed another drink at the bar, stepped outside, and shivered in the cool night air.

"I thought I was the only one unamused by the meal." A man stepped away from the side of the building and joined her at the railing overlooking the city.

She set down her drink on a bistro table and looked at him, surprised she hadn't noticed him in the room before. He was tall, with deep-set brown eyes and tousled ash-blonde hair. His shoulders were wide and his legs were long and she was wondering what he'd look like out of that tux.

That's the effect four flutes of champagne and one martini had on a girl the night before her mother was getting hitched. "You here alone?" she asked, skipping the small talk.

His eyes lingered on her rear, jutted back as

she leaned against the railing. He took his time finally bringing his gaze to meet hers with a sultry smile. "I am. And I hope to God you are, too."

She turned around and pressed her back against the railing, showing off her cleavage, enhanced by her strapless black gown. No need to be subtle when you knew what you wanted. "Listen. I'm having a really bad week and I'd like nothing more than to get out of here now. With you."

He tipped his head and looked at her, probably to determine if she was putting him on. "Just like that, huh?"

She nodded and snapped her fingers. "Just like that." She hoped she was improvising well; Carly wasn't the type to solicit men for a one-night stand. "I just need to let my friend know I'm leaving."

He reached out and brushed his thumb along her cheekbone. "I'll meet you in the lobby."

She shuddered at his touch and nodded, then lifted her gown off the floor and dashed back to the table. She squatted next to Tara's seat. "I found some one to make the weekend much more bearable. I'm leaving."

Tara's eyes widened. "Carly! I was kidding about picking up a guy for the night. You're not like that."

"Consider it my personal bachelorette party for my mom." She winked.

"Be careful!" she whispered.

"I'm picking up a guy at a charity ball. I'll be fine. You think they let criminals in here?"

"You better call me tomorrow!"

Carly walked away, looked over her shoulder, and fluttered her fingers. She certainly would not have been doing this without the amounts of alcohol she'd consumed. She'd been voted most responsible in high school and considered it a life-long assignment.

But tonight she was on sabbatical.

When she walked down the stairs to the lobby, she spotted her guy watching her. He pulled his hands out of his pockets and rubbed his chin, never taking his eyes off her.

The quiver in her belly told her this was a good plan, responsible or not. At age twenty-six, she'd never hooked up with a stranger. She took her time descending the stairs.

Her gown brushed the floor, rustling, as she walked to him. Soft classical music played overhead, and something tight and wild was unwinding in her belly. She looped her arm around his and squeezed his bicep. "Ready?" she asked in a husky voice.

"Where to?" he asked.

"My place. It's not far."

They walked outside and the breeze swirled her hair across her face. He brushed it away and left his fingers on her cheek. "What's your name?"

She took a deep breath and lied. "Samantha."

"I'm Clark. Nice to meet you." And he crushed his mouth against hers.

She woke the next morning with a pounding skull and a naked man in her bed; two things to which she didn't normally wake. And her head wasn't the only thing aching, she noticed, as she planted her feet on the floor. She looked at the clock and swore. It was eleven, and she had to be at the rehearsal luncheon at noon.

She staggered out of bed and pulled the sheets off Kent. Or was it Clark? Yes, Clark. "Come on, we've got to get up."

He groaned and rolled over, exposing his rear.

She paused for a moment to admire the view. Then she shook him by the shoulders.

He waved her away. "I'm spent, thanks to you. Let me sleep this off."

She climbed back in bed and tried to pull him up.

"You want more?" Rolling over on his side, he snagged her with one arm and pulled her to him. "It must have been a really bad week. But I'm glad to help."

Her lips found his again and she snaked her hands down his back until she reached the smooth peak of his buttocks. Yeah, she could do this again. Then she spotted the clock once more and pulled away. "And it's going to get even worse if I don't get up and get ready. I've got somewhere to be."

He sat up and looked at the clock. His eyes widened and he rubbed his face. "Me too." He hopped out of bed and picked his boxers off the floor. "Any idea where my pants are?"

She felt her cheeks flush. "Check the hall."

One eyebrow popped up. "Right. Now I remember."

She tied on her robe and wondered what the proper next day etiquette was for a one-night stand. She had no idea.

Clark came back in the room, buttoning his shirt.

She looked at him and gasped. "I'm sorry," she said, pointing to his neck.

He reached up to feel, and then turned to look in the mirror. "A hickey? I haven't had a hickey since junior high."

She giggled. "Sorry. Want some makeup to hide it?"

He buttoned his shirt up to his neck. "Does that cover it up?"

She nodded and tried to bite back her laughter. "So, should I make you eggs or something before you go? Toast?"

He laughed. "No. That's fine."

She gripped the banister on her four-poster bed. "Sorry, I've never done anything like this before."

He tried to hold back a grin. "I know."

She put her hands on her hips. "How?"

He shook his head, laughing. "Because I have. A lot." He finished buttoning his shirt. "I know a newbie when I see one."

She looked down at the floor, wondering if it was the moaning that had given her away.

He walked over and lifted her chin with a crooked finger. "Hey, it was a refreshing change to be with someone so...enthusiastic." He brushed his lips against hers.

She stepped back. "Well, thanks. Glad to have been of service." She turned him around by the shoulders, pushed his back, and marched him out of the room. "And have a nice life." She'd be far too embarrassed to ever see him again.

"Hey, you picked me up," he said, jogging down the stairs.

She tipped her chin in the air and crossed her arms. "No one forced you to come."

He held up his hands. "I'm not touching that one."

He didn't ask for her number and she didn't offer. It had been a wild, passionate night. But it was one she should soon forget, especially considering how smug he was being about the whole thing.

She led him to the front door and he turned around before leaving. "Samantha, that was great." He kissed her nose. "You're going to make some guy very happy some day."

"No, thank *you*. You made *me* very happy for one night. Now good-bye." She slammed the door behind him, still shocked by what she'd done. If she ever saw him again, she'd tell him what an arrogant, cocky womanizer he was.

Newbie. The word was going to haunt her. But there wasn't much time to stew in regret. She ran to the shower, and if she just dried her hair and put it up in a twist instead of curling it, she might get to the rehearsal brunch on time.

Everyone was outside by the gazebo when she arrived at the Blossom Reception Grove five minutes late. Her mother hurried over to her. "Come on. Wayne is very punctual," she said.

She'd met Wayne a few times and he was

nice enough. She was happy for her mother. Carly
was going to be her only attendant and felt guilty
for being late. "Sorry Mom, I had a charity thing
last night. I was out late." Images from the night
before swirled in her head. It really had been
quite incredible.

"Meet anyone interesting?"

She closed her eyes and swore she could still
feel his hands on her, the way his lips had
caressed her. Hell, she swore she could smell him.
"No, I didn't," she lied.

"Well, come over here. I want you to met
your new brother."

Sighing, she opened her eyes and saw Wayne
walking toward her.

With his arm around Clark.

*****

Shit, this is some kind of joke, right? He walked
over to Dad's new bride-to-be, Delilah, and her
daughter—the woman he'd just left, after a night
of Penthouse-worthy fun an hour earlier.

Her eyes were wide and her face was pale.
Her mother clapped. "Isn't this exciting? You
always wanted a brother, and now you have one!"

She didn't move. "What's wrong, Carly?" her
mother asked.

Carly? She'd given him a fake name!

She shook her head. "I have the feeling we've
met before. Clark, isn't it?"

Her mom frowned. "No, it's Rob. Wouldn't
that have been funny if you two knew each
other?"

He reached out his hand and did his best to
stifle a grin. "Nice to meet you, sis."

She took his hand and squeezed it hard. "Yes, very nice to meet you *Rob*."

"Carly, is it?" He rubbed his chin. "You don't look like a Carly to me."

They stood there staring at each other, and his father finally broke the silence. "Rob, you didn't need to get dressed up for the rehearsal. Why don't you take off your tie?"

Rob stepped back and straightened the knot at his throat. "No, I'm fine, Dad. I wasn't sure how casual this was going to be." He smoothed his tie down. "I'll leave it on."

Carly faked a cough, probably trying not to laugh about the hickey he was hiding.

"As you can see, Carly didn't do much with herself. I do hope you're planning to fix your hair before the reception, dear," her mother said, frowning.

Carly looked indignant. It was a cute look on her.

"I can give you a lift home, if you'd like," Rob offered.

Delilah set her hand on his arm. "What a wonderful gesture. It'll give you two a little time to get to know each other better. I want you two to be real close, just like a brother and sister." She looped her other arm through Carly's. "I'm so excited to start this new happy little family."

"I need a bathroom," Carly said with her hand over her stomach. She turned from him and tried to flee, but her mother pulled her back. "Honey, you and Rob are walking down the aisle together. Line up. The rehearsal's starting."

He held up his elbow to escort her and she

narrowed her eyes, then looped her arm through his. "Not one word," she hissed at him.

"I could never do something like that to my new sister."

She tried to step on his shoe, but he was too quick for her.

They lined up and waited for their cue. "I must say, you look even more radiant, although that could be due to all your blushing."

She smiled and talked through clenched teeth. "Shut up or I'll take your tie off."

The idea didn't seem half bad. Because even though the vixen from the night before was his new step-sister, that didn't do anything to stop the desire pounding through him to the beat of more, more, more.

He caught her stealing glances at him throughout the rehearsal. As bold as she had been in bed, she'd definitely hadn't been lying about not doing the one-night boogie very often. She seemed truly mortified the day after. And while she was trying to flash him nasty looks, he knew lust when he saw it. She was probably feeling as conflicted as he was.

And hopefully, just as horny, too.

She stalked off to the parking lot after lunch, and he chased after her. "Hey, I'm giving you a ride to your place."

"No need. I've got my car." She wouldn't face him.

He spotted her mother catching up to them. "Oh, good. I wanted to be sure you had time to fix yourself up a bit. Can you take her, Rob?'

"I can drive myself, Mom." She tucked a stray strawberry-blonde hair behind her ear.

Her mother dismissed the idea with the wave of her hand. "Take some time to get to know each other. You're family now."

He held open his passenger door for her. "Hop in, sis."

She got in and slammed the door, crossing her arms like a petulant tween.

He waited for her mother to wander away before he leaned over, wrapped his hand around the back of her head and kissed her. She pulled back for a moment, but then her mouth melted onto his with a moan as inspired as it had been the night before, although a bit quieter.

"Looks like I've still got the touch," he said, skimming his tongue along her jaw line.

She arched her head back "You're arrogant."

Nuzzling his nose along her neck, he laughed. "I know."

"And cocky," she said, whimpering as he bit her ear.

"Go on."

She wrapped hand around his head. "And a total playboy." She pulled away from him and looked out the window. "Leave before someone sees us."

"Whatever you want, Samantha."

Damn, it was a long fifteen-minute drive to her apartment.

*****

Carly couldn't believe she as returning to her place — with the man she'd pushed out just a few

105

hours earlier.

He walked in behind her, and slid his hand on her hips. He kissed the nape of her neck and then she froze, as he pulled the clip from her hair. "Need some help getting ready? I'd say we have two hours before we have to leave."

Her heart was pounding even harder than it had been the night before. She wanted to push him out the door again; but she wanted to pull him back into her bed even more.

She shook her head. "You're a pig-headed jerk. *And* you're my step-brother!" She wiggled her way out of his arms and stormed into the living room.

"Pig-headed jerk, maybe. But I'm not your step-brother yet." He followed her in and looked at his watch. "They won't be officially married for another few hours." He sat down on the couch and reached for her hand.

She couldn't resist. She set her palm on his and he pulled her down onto his lap. "If we do it again, I won't be a one-night stand. I'm sure that would make you feel better," he said.

He probably got whatever—and whoever— he wanted with that grin. She unzipped the back of her sundress. "Very persuasive, Clark. I guess one more time won't hurt."

He shimmied the dress off her and tossed it to the ground. "I just want make you happy again."

And he did make her very, very happy. They had half an hour to get back to the wedding site. She looked in the mirror and swore. "The whole point of me coming back here was to do my hair.

It looks even worse!" She tried fluffing it with her fingers and groaned. *Sorry Mom, my new brother raked my 'do out of place when he had me up against the wall?*

"Can I help?" he asked, pulling at the waistband of her panties as she stood in front of her vanity in the bedroom.

"Get out of here and stop being hot." She shooed him away with her hands.

"My clothes are in the car. I better go get dressed. Unless you think the folks would like this look." He turned around, modeling his striped boxers.

"Go!" she said, sliding her flat iron through her hair. "And stop calling them our folks." She closed her eyes and sighed. Her stepbrother. Of course he was her stepbrother.

Her mother tapped her wrist like she was checking an imaginary watch when the two of them walked into the church. The wedding started in twenty minutes, and Mom had wanted her there ten minutes ago.

Her mother tilted her head to look at her hairdo. "I thought you were going to fix your hair?"

Carly patted her head, back in an updo with an attempt at a few curls. "I tried, but, uh, my flat iron died on me."

Her mother pursed her lips. "Well, I hope you two had a chance to chat, at least."

Rob set his hand on Carly's shoulder. "We did. We really hit it off."

Carly rushed away from him with the

pretense of poufing the bottom of her mother's dress. It was white and flouncy with tiny pearl straps holding up the bodice. Far too young for her, but her mother glowed in it. "You look beautiful, Mom. You're a gorgeous bride." She stood up and smiled at her mother.

She set her hand on Carly's cheek. "And some day you will be too."

Carly rolled her eyes and smoothed her pale blue sheath.

"Hey, you never know when or where you're going to meet Mr. Right," she said.

"No, I only manage to meet Mr. Totally Wrong, again and again," Carly said, narrowing her eyes at Rob.

He cleared his throat, and Wayne came up between them. "Let's get a few family photos before the ceremony starts."

"Good. I just know I'm going to cry all my mascara off," her mother said.

Me too.

"Rob, get behind Carly, and set your hands on her shoulders."

"Sure thing, Delilah."

She squeezed his arm. "Call me Mom, dear."

"No!" Carly said, trying to lean forward away from Rob. "Don't."

"Honey, what's the matter? Rob is part of our family. I think you two should be thrilled to have each other, both of you being only children. Not anymore, though!" She clasped her hands together in glee. "I may be twenty odd years late, but I finally got you that baby brother you always wanted."

Carly quietly groaned and looked at him.
"I'm twenty-six. You're younger than me?"
He gave her a nice big grin. "Twenty-five.
This day just gets better and better." Rob settled
his hand on her shoulders and skated his thumb
along her collarbone while no one was looking.

She would have told him to knock it off, but
her throat was too tight.

After posing for pictures, they lined up in the
ballroom, ready to march down the gazebo. Rob
smiled at her. "How you holding up?"

She laughed nervously and twirled the
bouquet of pink roses in her hands. "I'll be feeling
a lot better when this day is over."

"We still have tomorrow to look forward to."

She faked a smile. "Right. Almost forgot.
The family picnic."

He winked at her. "I'll give you a ride there."

She closed her eyes and shook her head,
holding out her arm for him to take, all while
trying to ignore him — and the traitorous feelings
ballooning inside her. What had she done in a
past life to deserve this?

The ceremony was lovely, and her mother did
cry off much of her mascara. Carly had forgotten
to put hers on, so no problem there. In the
receiving line, she stood next to Rob, who
occasionally nudged the back of her knee with his
and brushed up against her whenever he could.
Perfectly obnoxious, just like she imagined a
stepbrother would be. That is, a stepbrother she'd
slept with.

"I'm going to kill you," she whispered, with a

tight smile.

"I'm telling Mom."

She jabbed him with her elbow.

She tried shaking him off most of the night, because she didn't know if she could remember not to wrap her arms around him in front of everyone who thought they were just brand new siblings. But he found her whenever she wandered off. After a very awkward dance in front of all their friends and family, they made their way outside to the gazebo where she finally took a deep breath.

"Seems like just yesterday I met you on a different starry night," he said, looking up at the sky. "Wait. That was yesterday."

"Hilarious."

He sat down on the floor of the gazebo and pulled her down next to him and they started it up all over again. He was more addicting than her daily Starbucks fix and exactly like her new favorite brew—she couldn't get enough, and she wanted nothing but.

She pulled away. "We've got to stop this."

He nipped at her for another kiss. "Why?"

That deserved an eye roll. "Because you annoy the hell out of me, and I don't feel like telling Mom I bagged my step-brother the night before her wedding."

He shrugged. "So we don't tell them. Makes it all that more exciting."

Damn. If only he wasn't such a good kisser. If only his chest wasn't so hard. If only his fingers weren't sliding off the straps of her dress, she might be able to walk away and say no.

But she couldn't even say no to a dish of Haagen Dazs vanilla bean. He was the whole tub with caramel, whipped cream and a cherry on top—and she was going to eat him without a spoon.

He kissed her shoulder and started to unzip her dress.

"Not here. Not now. We've got to get back," she whispered.

"When can we leave?"

Her lips throbbed and she should have told him she was going home alone. But for the first time in her life, lust took over her good sense.

"We'll leave after they cut the cake."

He pulled her up. "Then let's go get some cake and get out of here."

They walked back to the ballroom and her mother was coming toward the door, peering out into the sultry night. Carly flattened herself against the exterior stone wall of the ballroom while Rob stepped inside.

"Rob, have you seen Carly?" Her mother squinted at the dark gardens.

Carly winced; his shirttail was untucked in back.

Rob narrowed his eyes. "No, I haven't. I just stepped out for a breath of fresh air."

She sighed and grabbed Rob's hand. "I'm worried this whole night might be hard on her. Here I am getting married again and she hasn't had a boyfriend in months. Poor thing."

"She's a great girl. I'm sure she'll find someone just perfect."

"Thanks, Rob." She patted his hand and

dropped it. "It'll be nice for her to have a brother now to look out for her.

"Want me to go find her?"

"Would you? I'm about to throw the bouquet. Maybe it will be her lucky night." She crossed her fingers.

He grinned. "I'm sure it will be." He came back outside while her mother returned to the ballroom.

"Ready to come in?" he whispered.

"Poor, dateless Carly? Sure. Just let me search the bushes one more time for my dignity."

He yanked her up from the ground and kissed away her whine, while she tucked in his shirt.

She caught the bouquet, but only because her mother had run over and deposited it right into her hands. That earned a collective "Aww" from the guests, while Rob tried to hide his laughter.

She snagged a piece of cake to go and kissed her mother goodnight. "I'm beat. I'll see you tomorrow." Holding her shoes in one hand, she wondered what kind of massage job Rob could do on her feet.

"Make sure to say goodbye to Rob. I want you to be good friends."

She gulped and plastered on a big smile. "Whatever you say."

Rob followed her home and she dropped her cake on the kitchen table; where he proceeded to feed it to her and undress her at the same time.

"We really shouldn't be doing this."

He licked a smear of frosting off her chin.

112

"Why? You're never going to wear that dress again. Who cares if I get frosting on it?" She shook her head. "No. This. You know what I mean. It's weird." "I promised that you'd get lucky tonight. Can't go back on a promise." There was no use arguing. She'd never wanted to kiss someone so badly — and slug him at the same time. She imagined this was what it was like to be hooked on crack. At first, she'd thought it was just the thrill of bringing home a stranger the night before. But she wanted him even more now.

Even though he was the last possible person she should being doing this with.

And it was clear he wanted her too, as he kicked the chair out of the way and pulled off her stockings with his sticky, frosted fingers.

"Okay, we are not doing that again," she announced in bed the next morning, propped up on her elbow, staring at him.

"You're right. There's no time. I have to go home and get changed before this picnic."

She hopped out of bed and tied on her robe. "I mean this. Us."

He sat up. "Are you going to kick me out again?"

She shook her head and sat on the bed. "I should."

"That's not very sisterly of you."

She got up and paced the room. "Let's just forget this ever happened. You're my womanizing stepbrother. It was fun, but now it's done and we never speak of it again. Deal?"

Crossing his arms, he laughed. "Sure, it's a deal. If you can't stick to it."

She narrowed her eyes and threw a pillow at him.

*****

Rob spent most of his time with Carly at the picnic, under the pretense of introducing her to his side of the family. It was nearly impossible to keep his hands from sliding around her waist, or reaching over to take her mouth in his. He tried to keep an extra step away from her, but somehow, they always ended up right next to each other, shoulders brushing, hips bumping.

While grabbing drinks from the cooler for them, his cousin Troy approached him. "Dude, your new step-sister is hot."

He looked over at her, the breeze rustling her hair so that she had to push it off her face. He'd liked to grab a fistful of that silky hair, pull back her head and...

"Is she available?"

"Who? Carly?" He snapped his gaze away from her.

"Yeah, that would be cool, right? I mean she's no relation to me." Troy's lusty gaze had Rob curling up his fists.

Rob shook his head. "I think she's got a boyfriend."

"But she's here alone."

"Right. He's out of town." He nodded.

"Hey, let me know if that changes."

"Will do." *Not. Never. She's mine.* And that thought surprised the hell out of him.

He said goodbye to his Dad and Delilah, and wished them a good time on their honeymoon to Hawaii. They'd be gone for two weeks and he intended to use that time to get to know his stepsister better.

He found her before he left and gave her a quick brotherly hug. "Can I come over again?"

She pressed her eyes shut. Her head was shaking no, but the word *yes* slipped from her lips. "I'll meet you there in an hour."

He grabbed clothes so he could head to work the next morning from her place. He should have stopped to think about what he was doing. He hadn't been lying to Carly about having his share of one-nighters. He didn't do relationships well, and he didn't do them often. So what was it about her that was so different?

The fact that she was his stepsister didn't change anything. Hell, he'd found her before they even knew. But if this thing ended ugly, it would be messier than most. It's not like he could avoid her at family get-togethers.

Didn't matter. There was only one thing in the world he wanted right now, and that was her.

*****

A week later, Carly had to admit this was more than a fling. Several times she'd tried talking herself out of this. He'd conceded he was a dog when it came to women, and oh, yeah, he was her new baby brother. She had no idea how her mother would react to that bit of news. Certainly, it was a relationship with a short future. What if they ended up hating each other? Would their parents fight about who was at fault? Her mother would probably disown Rob if he dumped her.

She decided it might be best to let the relationship run its course—and keep the whole thing a secret from their parents.

They spent the entire two weeks together, going out to dinner and movies, playing Frisbee at the park. And they spent each night at his place or hers. She couldn't deny they were getting closer. She'd been hoping for her desire to fizzle out. But it only burned stronger.

Her nerves wound up as their parents' honeymoon wound down. "I'm not ready to tell them yet," she said, while they lounged on the couch at his place, watching a movie. "Let's be sure this is for real before we say anything."

"The last two weeks felt pretty real to me." He toyed with a piece of her hair. "We're going to have to tell them sometime."

Sighing, she leaned against him. "Not yet."

He kissed her. "You're the boss on this one."

Their parents were due back Sunday morning, so they stayed at Carly's for one last night together until they figured out their next move. Around noon, it seemed like a good time to get out of bed, but the doorbell rang. Carly ran to the bedroom window to see who was there. "It's my mother!"

She pulled on yoga pants and a shirt. "Get in the closet. I don't want her to find out like this."

He bolted out of bed and dashed for the door, closing it behind him.

She ran to let her mother in and was greeted with hugs, kisses, and boxes of chocolate macadamia nuts and other goodies from Oahu.

"I missed you so much!" her mom said. "I had to come right over and catch up. What's new?"

"Um, not much." She scratched her head.

"Now that can't be true. Let's go to lunch and I'll tell you all about our trip." She frowned at Carly. "But you need to do something with yourself. You look like you just got out of bed. You're not even wearing a bra," she whispered. "Go on upstairs. We'll talk while you get ready."

Carly froze, but there was no stopping her mother, who was half way up the stairs already. She chased her into the room, and her mother frowned at her bed, then stripped off the sheets. "You really need to clean up the place."

Carly grimaced. "I can get those, Mom. Really."

"Nonsense. You talk while I clean."

Carly slunk into the bathroom to wash her face and brush her teeth. "I'll be real quick." She dug out her makeup and got to work.

"We had a wonderful time in Hawaii. But I must say, the food at the luau was horrible. Where do you keep your sheets, honey? In the closet here?"

Carly ran out, brandishing her hairbrush. "No! In the hall." She set her hand on her chest, trying to calm her heart.

Her mother's eyes widened. "What, you think I haven't seen your messy closet before?" She went out into the hall and raised her voice. "So, I guess Rob's seeing someone."

Her heart dropped for a moment, but she realized it couldn't be true; she'd been spending all her time with Rob. "Who?" Her voice cracked.

"Some Samantha person. Maybe he met her at the wedding. Is that a friend of yours?"

She fought back a smile. "No."

She snapped the sheet open over the bed. "Well, he talked with his father a few times while we were on vacation and told him he's crazy about her."

"Really?"

Nodding, she slipped a pillow into a new case. "Which is remarkable, because I guess he's quite the ladies' man. Who knows, maybe you'll be in another wedding soon."

Carly put on her bra and shirt in the bathroom while her mother chattered away. "I just wish you could meet someone."

"I did."

Her mother dropped the pillow. "Who?"

She looked at herself in the mirror, satisfied with her quick fix-up. "Clark. I met him at the charity ball the night before your wedding."

Her mother rushed over and hugged her. "Oh, that's such good news. I was starting to worry about you. Is it serious?"

She glanced at the closet. "We can talk about this over lunch."

"No. You sit down and tell me all about it now." She pulled her onto the freshly made bed.

"Well, he's very good looking. And nice."

"Oh, skip that business, is he good in bed?"

Carly started choking. "Mother, that's not something I want to talk about with you."

Her mom gave her a playful push. "Darling, you're not a little girl anymore. You're in a relationship, why not talk about it? Wayne and I

118

got this wonderful lovemaking book as a wedding gift: *365 Positions of Passion*. I could lend it to you. Although we've only gotten through the first twenty-five."

Carly heard a groan from the closet.

"What was that?" her mom asked.

Carly rubbed her belly. "My stomach. I'm hungry. Let's go."

"Put on something nicer than that." She stood up and headed for Carly's closet.

"No! I've got a jacket downstairs."

Her mother opened the door. "Where's that nice cardigan I got you? And what in the world did you do in here?" She pointed to the mound of clothes on the floor.

Carly rushed over and pulled the sweater off its hanger. "I was sorting through some things. Let's go." She slammed the closet door shut and led her mother downstairs.

*****

Rob waited until he heard the car pull away to climb out of the closet. His knees hurt like hell from being curled up in a ball under the clothes he'd pulled off the shelves behind him. He held up a slinky blue shirt that probably looked damn sexy on Carly.

Heading for the bathroom, he thought about washing his ears out after their discussion of 365 passionate positions. But hearing Carly say she was really into him made it all worth it. He got dressed and left her a note to meet him at his place.

Two hours later, Carly showed up on his doorstep.

He kissed her and led her inside. "Hey, Samantha. Where's Clark?"

"Very funny."

"Why did you make up a boyfriend? Isn't that going to make it harder to tell her the truth about us?"

"I know. I panicked. But I'm glad to hear you like Samantha so much." Her big grin delighted him.

"You know me, the womanizer. Juggling the two of you has been hard."

She gave him a look that threatened no fun later unless he knocked it off.

The doorbell rang, interrupting his plans to pull her into the bedroom.

"Maybe it's Samantha. Be right back." He dashed to the front door, unlocked the deadbolt and found his father and Delilah on the other side carrying Panama Jack bags from Hawaii. "Dad, Delilah!" *Guess this is how they find out.* "What a surprise!"

"Hi, Rob," his father said. "Your stepmother just couldn't wait to bring you some of the goodies we got on our honeymoon." They walked in without exactly being invited.

"Yes, I visited Carly earlier —" she looked up, surprised. "Carly?"

Carly said nothing and just held one hand up in greeting. He was waiting for her to spill the beans, but she kept her mouth clamped tight.

Her mother's eyes darted back and forth between the two of them and Rob figured she was working out exactly what was going on. A big smile unfurled on Delilah's face. "I'm so glad to see you spending time together. This is working out just like I hoped it would. How does it feel to have a sister after all these years?"

Rob rubbed the back of his neck. "Different than I expected. But nice."

Carly nodded in agreement. "I should go. Thanks for inviting me over."

"Don't you want to stay and get the folks caught up on everything?" he asked with a big smile.

She shook her head, no.

Delilah grabbed Carly's hand and led her over to the couch. "Yes, stay, honey. We just got here."

"Please sit down," Rob said. "Let me get us some wine." *It might help us all.*

"How's your girlfriend, Samantha?" Delilah asked.

Rob caught his breath. "Oh, she's good. Real good."

Delilah clapped. "That's so exciting. Carly has a new boyfriend, too. We should all go out together. Wouldn't that be fun?"

He almost dropped the wine glass he was filling. "Sure. We'll have to do that sometime. A few months from now or something." Why wasn't Carly speaking up?

"How about this Friday?" she asked.

He rubbed the back of his head. "I will have to check with her. With Samantha." Damn, they should just get it out in the open now before they dug themselves in deeper. But he wasn't going to be the one to do it. He wanted to be sure Carly felt comfortable enough to share the news.

"Good. Carly, do you think Clark can make

our triple date?"

"I'll have to see," she stammered.

Delilah pulled out her cell and punched in the information. "Good. Let's say Friday at six."

"So, what's this Samantha like?" his dad asked. "Pretty?"

"She's beautiful." He handed Carly her glass of wine and got caught in her gorgeous green eyes that looked scared as hell.

"And in bed?"

He looked down at the floor. "Um, not in front of the ladies, Dad."

"Oh, Wayne. Tell him about our book."

Rob held up his hand. "I don't want to hear about the book. Please."

They stayed for an hour, and when he closed the door behind them, Carly started gathering her things. "I've got to go. I can't do this anymore."

He snaked his arms around her waist, but she pushed her way out of his embrace.

He sighed. "Let's just tell them the truth. We're dating. Is it that big of a deal?"

Collecting the empty wine glasses from the room, she shook her head. "My mother calls you her son. I don't want to ruin things for them. They just got married. And when we break up, they'll blame each other, it'll be horrible."

He took her by the shoulders. "Are you sure this is really about our parents?"

"Of course it is."

He took her hand. "I think you might be afraid we really do have something special going on. And it scares you enough to send you running."

She let her fingers slide from his and headed for the door. She looked back at him. "I'm sorry. It's been fun. That's what I asked for, right?"

"Take the time you need to sort this out. Just tell me when you're ready. I'm not going anywhere."

She wouldn't look at him. "I can't." And she walked out the door.

*****

Carly missed him so much it hurt. Two weeks had passed since she'd last seen him. She'd been dodging her mother's requests to bring Clark along for a triple date. She hadn't had the heart to tell her she'd broken up with Clark. Her mother had been easing off the suffocating concern ever since Carly "got a boyfriend" but she could only put her off so long.

Rob's words haunted her, though. She wasn't entirely sure why she'd been so spooked. Maybe having the four of them in the room together had been too much. The whole thing had "mistake" written all over it.

She finally agreed to come to dinner, and planned on showing up without her date. She wondered how Rob was going to handle "Samantha." The two of them had to get used to just being friends in front of their folks. This was an important first step.

She put on her best little black dress, blew out her hair and wondered why she was bothering.

Her mother peered behind her expectantly when she walked in the restaurant. "Where's your date?"

Rob stood up and pulled out her chair for her. She sat down and said, "He got called to an emergency meeting."

"Well, poor Rob here has been dumped. Can you imagine? The nerve of that girl!" Her mother patted his hand.

Carly looked up at him under her lashes. "What happened?"

"Things were going so well that she got spooked and ran."

"Is that the most ridiculous thing you've ever heard?" her mother asked.

Carly swirled her wine and took a drink—a very long drink.

"You'll find someone else, don't worry," his father said.

He finished off his beer and set it down. "Yeah, but I really liked Samantha. I thought we had a shot at it."

Carly stood up. "I need to use the restroom." Locking herself in a stall, she tried to gain her composure. Should she just tell her mother she and Rob were a couple? But what if it didn't work out? That could really drive a wedge between her mom and Wayne. The situation still seemed too impossible to consider.

She went back to the table but couldn't eat much of her dinner. She was too aware of Rob's eyes on her, remembering every touch, every place they'd made love.

As Wayne fished out his credit card to pay the bill, her mother planted a big kiss on Rob's cheek. "If she means that much to you, I think you should go after her."

"Really?"

Rob looked at Carly. "What do you think I should do?"

She looked at her half-eaten plate of food. "Sometimes, things just aren't meant to be."

Her mother nudged her shoulder. "Hey, show your brother a little more support."

"You're right. Sorry, brother." Carly stood up. "I have to go. Thanks for dinner."

Rob was at her door half an hour later. She opened it a crack. "Please go home. It's pointless to prolong things. You're my step-brother now, and we'll just have to be happy with the memories."

"Are you sure? I don't want to push you, but I don't want to give up on you, Carly."

She nodded. "I'm sure." She didn't let him say another word before she closed the door on him. She peeked out the window and watched him shuffle back to his car. He sat there for a while before driving away.

She looked in her freezer and realized there was no amount of chocolate or ice cream to deal with this heartache. She went to bed and wrapped herself in her bedspread, trying to find a whiff of his scent.

But every trace of him was gone.

Her mother called with an invitation to Wayne's birthday party the following Saturday night. Wayne had sold his condo and moved into her childhood home with her Mom. It was their first big shindig as a married couple.

"I can't. I have plans with Clark."

"Oh, honey. Your stepfather will be so disappointed. Please? Bring Clark. This is our first family event together. We want both our children there."

Carly was quiet and finally gave in. It's not like she'd be able to avoid Rob for the rest of her life. "I'll see what I can do."

She was tempted to dress up, but what was the point? She settled on jeans and a sweater and fussed just a little with her hair and makeup. If she were lucky, Rob had met someone new.

She walked into her mother's house and spotted him right away. Their eyes locked, and she ran her fingers over her lips. The person he was talking to turned around to see who had captured Rob's attention, so she scooted to the kitchen away from his view.

"Darling!" Mom rushed over and gave her a hug. "Where's Clark?"

"He couldn't come."

"That's too bad," Rob said behind her.

She jumped. "Oh, hello."

"Rob's solo, too. Guess it's a good brother-sister bonding night," her mother said.

"Maybe we'll play Twister," Rob said.

"Good idea," said her mother. "I'm off to mingle. Have fun you two!" She left them alone in the kitchen.

"How have you been?" He reached for her hand.

She stepped back and tried to force a smile, but she felt tears coming instead, so she turned around. "Not so great."

He ran his fingers down her hair and rested them on her shoulder. "Me neither. I really miss you."

She nodded. They heard someone coming and stepped apart.

It was her mother. "Honey, I forgot to suggest you should give him a tour of the house. He's never been here before." She shooed them out of the room.

Carly gulped and led the way. "Well, you've seen the kitchen. The family room's packed with people as you can see." She led him through the crowded room into the empty dining room and then the living room. "Exciting stuff," she said, as they stopped in front of the fireplace.

He pointed to the stairs. "I suppose the bedrooms are up there."

She nodded, hoping she could control herself around him once they were up there alone.

He followed her up and she showed him her mother's and Wayne's room, the guest room and the bathroom, and then her old bedroom. "And this is where I lived for eighteen years." She pushed the door open and led him inside. The same flowered pink wallpaper covered the room, and her white canopy bed sat in the same place. Her pictures and posters from high school still hung on the walls.

"'N Synch. Really?" he teased, pointing to one of her posters. He looked around, smiling. "It's like a Carly shrine." He closed the door behind them. "I've missed you. So much." He held out his hand. "Come here."

Stepping back and pressing her back

127

against the wall, she tried to protest. He came to her, twining his fingers through her hair.

Her insides tumbled as he touched her. She sucked in a deep breath. "I've been miserable without you. Let's tell them. Whatever happens, happens."

His hands moved down to her shoulders and he pulled her into a hug. "Thank God." He kissed her.

Tears stung her eyes as she squeezed his arms. "We'll tell them after the party. It'll be easier after a few drinks."

"I'll follow your lead."

His tongue was skating a swirling path across her lips when the door opened. "Kids, it's time for cake…" Her mother's voice trailed off, and they pushed off the wall, rearranging their clothing and hair.

She dropped her wine glass. "What are you two doing?" she asked in a whisper.

Rob stood up. "Delilah…"

Wayne walked in the room behind her. "Did you find them?" He did a double take. "What's going on up here?"

Her mother's mouth flapped open and closed, but nothing came out.

"She caught us kissing," Carly said.

"It was more than that," he mother shot back. "What about Clark? You told me you loved him and you're cheating on him? You said he could be the one! And you're with your…your…" She couldn't get the words out and she pressed her eyes shut.

Rob looked at Carly. "You love Clark?"

She nodded and leaned into his chest. Rob kissed her head. "And I love Samantha."

Her mother's chest was heaving. "So then why are you kissing...your sister?

"Stepsister, mother. We're not related, and Rob is Clark."

Her mother straightened up and cocked her head. "What?"

Carly nodded. "I met Rob the night before your wedding and we..." she bit her lip. "Let's just say I was very surprised to find out he was my new brother the next day."

Rob wrapped his arms around her from behind. "And Carly is Samantha."

Carly shrugged. "He was my lover before he was my brother."

"Why didn't you tell us?" Wayne asked.

"We weren't sure it was more than a fling. We didn't want to cause a rift between you two if things didn't work out."

Rob nodded. "But it's definitely working out."

Her mother stood there in a daze. "I never imagined..." She shook her head and shrugged. "I guess...I guess it's fine. No, it's great."

Carly ran to her and grabbed her arms. "Are you sure? I don't want this causing problems with you and Wayne."

"Hey, if you keep Rob from moping around like he's been the past few weeks, I'm all for it," Wayne said.

"It'll make for an interesting family photo," her mother said quietly, reaching to hold the door for support.

"What are you going to tell people?" Carly asked.

"That our kids fell in love?" She threw up her hands.

"And we might as well go tell everyone now since most of the family's here," Wayne said.

Carly's eyes went wide. "Now?"

They walked into the dining room, where everyone was gathered to watch Wayne blow out the candles on his cake. The room hushed and he looked at the crowd and smiled. "Want to know my birthday wish?"

"Yeah, sure!" called out a few people.

He pulled Carly and Rob over to stand next to them. "I wish nothing but happiness for our children, Rob and Carly."

The crowd interrupted with an awww before he could continue. "Because apparently, these two have fallen in love."

No one said anything. Then Rob kissed Carly's cheek and someone whistled. Then other people joined in, hooting and hollering and clapping, and there was some whispering, too, of course.

He dipped her for a dramatic kiss and the cheering continued.

Then Wayne blew out his candles.

"Hope that wish comes true," Rob whispered to Carly.

"It already has," she said.

They excused themselves to leave early. "It'll give everyone a chance to gossip," she told her mother.

Her eyes twinkled. "Yes, I'm sure that's why you're leaving early. Want me to get that book I was telling you about?"

Carly looked at the floor. "Good night, Mother!"

The following spring, they lined up to walk down the aisle outside the Blossom Reception Grove on a warm, May night.

"You here alone?" he asked her.

She grinned. "Not for long." She rubbed her damp hands together and looked up at Rob. "But I'm nervous. I've never done this before."

He kissed her head. "I can tell. Total newbie."

She whacked him with her bouquet and her mother turned around with a glare. "You two kids knock it off."

They giggled and kissed. "Mom loves me better," Carly teased.

"But no one loves you more than me." He kissed her, and she blessed the bad karma that had sent nothing but losers her way until she had found the most unlikely match.

"I told you that you'd make some guy very happy some day."

She grinned and walked down the aisle with the last person she ever expected. Only a responsible girl like her would turn a one-night stand into the romance of her life.

"Desperately Seeking Cupid"
By Lisa Scott

Scanning the room one more time at the Blossom Reception Grove, I lowered my expectations from meeting a hot guy, to scoring an extra slice of wedding cake—with a big honking flower on top. Any good looking man I spotted had a date or a wife. It was clear the hundred-fifty dollars I'd shelled out for my new dress would've been better spent on a month's worth of gourmet chocolate. Or buckets of coffee. At least I'd gotten it on sale.

I scowled at my seating card: Brianna Keller and guest; guest had been crossed off. With no one to bring and not a prospect in sight, I was stuck at the single girl's table. Only, all of the "girls" around me were more like the Golden Girls than the Gilmore Girls. I loved my Grandma, but I didn't want to hang out with her peeps when I was supposed to be meeting men—preferably, born in the same decade as me. They seemed to be lovely ladies, but not exactly the wingman material needed for scoping out dates.

"I said, Carly was my next door neighbor growing up," I told the white-haired woman sitting next to me, wearing a big peacock brooch. She'd already asked me three times how I knew the bride.

"She looks younger than you," said another lady, who was draped in rhinestones and squinting at the bride.

I faked a big smile. "She is." And getting

married first, the nerve of her. How many times had I slipped her contraband makeup on the bus ride to school? I showed her how to put on false eyelashes, for crying out loud. And this is how she repays me?

"Now, why don't you have a date, dear?" one of the other women asked me. Her water glass had a big red lip print on it. This was like my weekly phone conversation with my mother. Only, I had lied to her about my date for the wedding and said the "new guy" I was seeing couldn't make it.

"Well...um...that's a good question." I stammered, unwrapping one of the personalized Hershey's kisses the couple left as favors. This was going to be a long summer if I didn't find decent date-material—I was invited to six more weddings over the next three months. My fake boyfriend couldn't miss them all, and my mother would be at a few of them.

"You're so pretty. I just don't understand why you don't have a boyfriend," peacock-brooch woman said. Her eyes widened. "Wait, you're not a Libertarian, are you?"

"Mildred!" Her friend in the rhinestones smacked her with her purse.

I chased the chocolate with the rest of my wine. "No, I'm actually Independent in more ways than one, and I like men. A lot." My last real relationship had been three years ago. Nick and the co-worker he cheated on me with were now married. So much for Karma being a bitch. "I just can't find the right one." At this point, I'd even settle for Mr. Could-Be-Should-Be-Might-Be-

Right.

"What about those dating websites I see on TV all the time?" asked another woman, wearing a ruffled, lavender crepe dress.

"Tried three of them. No luck. I've agreed to set-ups. Blind dates." I counted the lame attempts on my fingers. "I've even done speed dating."

Lavender-dress-lady's eyes popped open. "Oh dear, you shouldn't turn to barbiturates. Drugs aren't the answer. Just say no." She nodded emphatically.

Pressing my eyes closed, I smiled. "Speed dating is a really quick date with a bunch of men."

Their eyes went wide, and Red Lips whispered, "We had a name for that kind of girl in my day…"

"You were that kind of girl," Lavender said to Red Lips. That earned another purse whack from Rhinestones.

I gulped another mouthful of Chardonnay. "I'd probably have a date if I *was* that kind of girl." I dropped my head in my hands. "I've tried everything. I swear cupid's given up on me." The wine was making me whiney. I needed to stop and remember all the good things in my life: great friends and family, a speedy metabolism, my job in sales for an educational software company that allowed leisurely lunches I could then write off. Seriously, all good stuff.

"Maybe you need to make some changes in your life," Rhinestones kindly suggested.

"Like your hair. Are you a real redhead? I've never seen that shade before," another lady asked, putting on the glasses that hung around her neck, then examining me.

I rubbed my temples. "I spend a lot of time at the hairdresser." I changed my hair color more often than I swapped out new lipstick shades.

"Me, too," said another lady. Her short, bobbed hair had a strange blue tint to it. Sitting between her and the white-haired woman, we must have looked like the American flag.

"Maybe something more natural would be appealing to the gentlemen?" Peacock suggested, nodding encouragingly.

"Ettie, Patsy — leave her alone. She's beautiful just the way she is." An older blonde-haired woman waved the idea away with a sweep of her hand. "Women today don't need a man to be happy. Wish I'd known that back in the day."

The ladies laughed, but I pouted. "Actually, I really do want a man," I said quietly.

The gals each let out little sounds of pity. And really, that didn't help at all.

The blonde woman shook her head. "I'll bet your feng-shui is all off."

The other ladies murmured. "Oh, of course. You're probably right, Virginia," said Red Lips. "It must be bad feng shui. You'll never land a man if you're feng shui isn't right." She shook her head and tsk-tsk'd. "You need to get that adjusted."

I gulped. "I'm pretty sure my gynecologist would have noticed that at the last checkup."

The ladies giggled and Virginia whooped with laughter. "Feng shui isn't a sex thing, it's all about the energy flow in your home."

"I live in an apartment. Not much room for anything to flow."

She wagged a shiny, red-tipped finger at me. "Doesn't matter if you live in a cardboard box. The types of things you have in your home and the way they're arranged affect how energy flows through your life. There's so much you can do to change your situation." She fished a business card out of her purse. "I'm a feng shui consultant, among other things. Give me a call and I can see what's going on in your apartment." She cocked an eyebrow. "I'll bet you've got big problems in your relationship bagua."

I took the card. "I didn't even know I had a relationship bagua," I said meekly.

The ladies laughed again. "Virginia really knows her stuff," Blue Hair said with a brisk nod. "When she straightened up my prosperity bagua, I found an old life insurance policy my husband had tucked away in a book." She crossed herself. "God rest his soul." She shrugged. "Took a cruise to Alaska with the money."

Lavender reached over and patted my hand. "You just don't have your things in the right place, that's all. Since Virginia fixed my place up, I haven't been able to keep the men away," she said with a giggle.

And that's when a silver-haired man approached the table and said to her, "Dance with me, or you'll break my heart, which would be a shame considering I just got the old ticker fixed." He patted his chest.

She gave him a coy smile. "I knew I bought a new pair of dancing shoes for a good reason." She stood up and they shuffled off to the dance floor. Virginia looked at me. "She's not kidding."

But feng shui? It sounded like something I'd avoid on the menu at my favorite Thai restaurant, not something that could turn my love life around. I looked at the couples gathering on the dance floor, and then at the few of us solo guests left alone at the tables. I snatched Lavender's Hershey's kisses. She was too busy whooping it up to notice.

I spent the rest of the reception chatting with the ladies, exchanging Facebook information and Twitter ID's. I kept an eye out for any single men that I might have missed. There were a few – in their seventies. My new gal pals had a stream of dance partners. I had to battle them on the dance floor as we lined up to grab the bouquet; Rhinestones caught it and waved it over her head in a victory celebration, the show off. I waited for my two pieces of cake and went home depressed. I stood in my apartment, wondering where my relationship bagua was, and if it came with a warranty because mine was certainly broken.

"How was the wedding?" my mother asked on the phone the next day. She and my stepfather were spending the month in North Carolina visiting his new grandchild. No pressure there.

"It was nice."

"Did you meet anyone?" Mom asked.

Here we go. "Seven nice senior citizen ladies. I told you, I've got a boyfriend. Charles just couldn't come. I wasn't looking to meet anyone."

If she knew how desperate I was, she'd probably fly home and start lining up blind dates for me in some pathetic bachelor draft event.

I was only twenty-seven, but she was ready to pay someone to date me. When she was my age, she liked to remind me, she'd been married twice. It killed her that I didn't have the same inborn mate-finding genes. Neither did my half brother. Only, he was smart enough to move to Alaska—and work as a long-haul trucker where he was unreachable five days out of seven. *Maybe I should see if they have any openings. There are tons of single guys in Alaska, right?*

"Well, I just can't wait to meet this Chuck at your cousin Emily's wedding. I don't hope he'll be busy *that* day, too."

"He's a bar manager. It's tough to get weekend's off." At least I had been born with good fibbing genes. "But he'll try his best."

"Wait, I thought he was a restaurant manager?"

Okay. Not that good of a liar. "Uh, they have a bar and a restaurant. He got a promotion. They gave him a big plaque and everything."

She was quiet for a moment. "I just don't have a good feeling about this one, honey. I just don't hear the excitement in your voice."

"Don't worry, Mom." *And next, I'll tell the grass to stop growing.* I hung up and the phone rang five minutes later.

"How was the wedding?" my best friend, Sarah, asked.

I fell back on my bed. My friends and family seemed even more desperate for me to meet someone than I did. It just made me more panicked about the whole thing. "Eh, it was okay."

"I bet that dress was a killer." She had helped me pick it out and guaranteed it would be a success. Then, we found two more to rotate through the rest of the weddings. I swear, if I wasn't snacking, I was shopping. I did both things very well.

I planted my feet on the wall. This all felt very junior high, like I was recounting the dance I'd gone to the night before. I never had much to report back then, either. "The reception was depressing, but the cake was good. I might order one from the same bakery and eat the whole thing myself."

"You won't fit into your dresses and you've got six more weddings to go to," she said in an obnoxious, singsong voice.

"I could always cancel. Every wedding has its no shows."

Her sigh was long and exasperated. "You're coming out with me tonight."

I closed my eyes. "I don't want to go to another bar. Unless it's a chocolate bar."

"You're right. Stay home. Someone will probably just come knocking on your door."

I sighed. She was right. "You are not as nice as you look, you know."

"You've been talking to my exes."

"I'm not wearing thongs anymore," I said to Sarah as we scooted off the dance floor. "Especially not if I'm going to be dancing." I winced. "If a guy won't love me with panty lines, he's not worth it." I'd spent an hour getting ready, sliding into clothes that actually hurt—for what? Accidental groping on the dance floor by guys five years younger than me? I tucked my hair behind my ears and looked around the room hopelessly. "I'm going shopping for new undies Monday. Wanna come?"

"Oh, stop," Sarah said. "You're a thong girl and you know it."

We headed for the bar. "It's kind of false advertising when you think about it, because if I do get together with someone, I will certainly stop wearing them. Why lead them on, right? Honesty. That's the best policy."

A dark-haired guy appeared next to me, grinning.

Well, this is an interesting development. I smiled back.

"There's another option. You could wear no underwear at all," he said. "And maybe add your bra to the collection up there." He pointed to the jungle of bras hanging above bar.

Ah yes. My loser-magnet must have fired up. I groaned. "So that's your method? Eavesdrop and then slide in cheeky comments?"

One corner of his mouth quirked up. "Cheeky, definitely cheeky, especially without the underwear. Why not go take yours off and try it out? It'll make things easier when I take you home later."

I rolled my eyes and looked at Sarah. "There's gotta be a late night bakery around here with cupcakes, right?"

Recovering from my sugar hangover Sunday morning, I did some cleaning up. I put away my dress and shoes, and cleaned out my clutch. I pulled out Virginia's card. "Virginia Collins: Interior Decorating and Feng Shui Consultant." I fiddled with the card. "What the hell." I dialed her number. What did I have to lose?

"Virginia, it's Brianna Keller. We met at the wedding Friday night? I'd really like to hire you to check out my feng shui problems."

"I'm so glad you called. You'll be amazed what a few simple changes in your home will do."

We made an appointment for the following Saturday afternoon. After meeting an engaged man at a bar Thursday night who was looking for a "special friendship" until he got married — and maybe afterwards, too — and then bumping into a businessman in town looking for company on Friday night, I decided I didn't need to make some *little* changes in my life; I needed to make some *huge* changes — fast. I was thrilled I'd made the appointment to meet her. *It couldn't make things worse. Right?*

"Oh, dear," she said when she walked through my door. The smell of flowery perfume followed her in.

I twisted my hands in front of me. "It's that bad? You can tell already?" Was I like one of those women who walked around with a bad highlighting job and didn't know it?

She walked over to the fireplace and pointed

141

to the huge picture hanging over the mantle. "You're sending the universe the wrong signals, dear. If you want to be part of a couple, you shouldn't be displaying artwork featuring a sad, single woman! That's what you're drawing into your world."

I looked at the watercolor I'd purchased at an art festival a few years back. "She's dreamy, not sad."

"She's pathetic."

I stepped back and tilted my head. "Wistful?"

Virginia scrunched up her nose and shook her head. "Wretched."

I stared at the painting and realized she did look as if she was thinking about ending it all. *Ugh. She looks like me!* I flopped into a chair. "So, what do I do?"

"Take it down. Put up a picture that shows a couple, or at least a pair of something. Nothing singular. And this candle?" She picked up an old jar candle I had sitting on the mantle. "You need two candles, not just one sitting up here. If you want to be a pair, you have to send that idea out to the universe. Heck, put a bowl of pears in your kitchen. Right now, you're practically begging the universe to keep you single."

"This here is what's been causing all my problems? My relationship bagua?" I gestured to the family room.

"No, that's the rear right corner of your home. But if you've got all of these solitary symbols in your home, that's a big problem, too." She scribbled something in her notebook.

"The back right corner, huh? That's where my

bedroom is," I said.

"Let's go have a look at the damage."

I led her to the room and wondered what she'd see. My antique sleigh bed sat against the far wall, along with a matching dresser, a nightstand with a light and a desk with my computer on top. It seemed simple enough to me. How could *this* be impacting my love life?

She frowned and shook her head. "No wonder. Remember what I said about pairs of things? You need two nightstands and two lamps. And get the computer out of here—unless you want a relationship only with your work. You need symbols of love and romance in here. Some pink roses and pink quartz."

She flung open my closet. "Whoa. Can one woman wear all those clothes in a year? Clear some space in here, like you're expecting to share it with someone." She winked at me.

We went through the house moving things and making a pile of stuff that had to go for sure. Like the lonely lady painting. And my unicorn collection from seventh grade, just in case one horn was a bad omen, too.

Turns out, I had things lined up perfectly in my career bagua, but apparently the money would roll in if I added a few purple items in my prosperity bagua. That was in the rear left of my apartment. I took notes as she made her way through.

"First things first. You need to clear out all the clutter." Virginia swept her arm across the apartment. "Do a thorough cleaning first, so your energy can get moving in here again."

"Cleaning?" Ugh.

She nodded.

A girl's gotta do what a girl's gotta do. "I'll get right on it."

She smiled. "Don't worry. It's not all hard work. You've got some shopping to do, too. There's a terrific store on Main Street that I send clients to," Virginia said. "Interior Inspirations, it's called."

I clapped. "Now we're talking the same language. Shopping. That's something I can do."

"Good. Let me come back in two weeks and see if things haven't changed some. And then we'll figure out what you need to do next." She headed for the door. "Oh, and the girls are doing brunch at the Parkside Bistro today. They really liked you. We've got reservations at noon if you'd like to come. We do it every Sunday — and we don't let just anybody into our group, you know."

But I was too busy to join them. I had so much cleaning and clutter busting to do. Once I got started, I was on a roll, discarding four of the six red camisoles I had purchased — five of which had never been worn. I downsized my shoe collection from sixty-four pairs to thirty-one. Baby steps.

By three o'clock Sunday afternoon, I was energized and ready to make some changes. I felt more confident already. I grabbed my purse and headed for the store Virginia had recommended. How often does a girl get assigned a shopping trip? I smiled up at the sun as I walked down the sidewalk, beaming at everyone who passed. Who knows? Maybe the men would just start falling from the sky — and I needed to be at my friendly best when they dropped at my feet. Perhaps my next boyfriend was right there on the street. I found the store, and bells chimed on the door when I entered. Soothing music played overhead and the smell of spicy incense hit me.

The place was packed with shelves of vases and statues. Gorgeous pictures hung on the walls, and cute antique chairs and tables were scattered around the room, arranged in stylish setups. I went right to a long shelf lined with candleholders on a lace runner, and picked a beautiful crystal set for the bedroom and a marble pair for the mantle. I took them up to the counter.

A man was finishing up a sale with a customer. "Can I help you?" he asked. His bright blue eyes caught me off guard. Not my type, but there was something about him that made me gulp.

I took a deep breath and set my purchases on the glass counter top. "I'm going to take these, but I've got a few more things to buy." I pulled out my list and scanned the items I needed to add to makes things right in my home. "Where are your lamps?"

"Back of the store. Let me show you." He slid out from behind the counter. He was tall and lanky, yet very masculine, with a strong, stubbled jaw. I watched his dirty-blonde ponytail bounce as I walked behind him. I tried to imagine what he'd look like clean-shaven with a crisp haircut, like most of the guys I dated. I just couldn't picture it.

145

"I'm Zach Johnson." He offered his hand.

"Brianna Keller." His handshake was surprisingly firm. The rest of him looked firm, too.

"Did you have something particular in mind?" he asked, interrupting my train of thought that involved him minus a shirt.

I blushed. "What?"

"The lamp. Are you looking for inspiration to hit, or did you have something in mind?"

"Right. The lamp." I looked at my notes and took a deep breath. "Something neutral, in earth tones." I walked through the store, running my fingers over beautiful lamp bases and gorgeous shades. Zach followed me. I picked up one in a creamy silk color and it was love.

"Do you have another one of these?" I asked. "I need two."

"Let me check in back." He smelled good as he walked past me.

I scanned the shop and spotted a stack of framed prints. Sorting through them, I chose a watercolor of a couple holding hands, strolling the beach at sunset. *That's what I want.* That would be going right over my mantle.

Zach returned from the storeroom, frowning. "I don't have another one of those lamps in stock, but I can order it for you."

"Great, and I'll take this picture. Oh, and do you have any rose quartz?"

He pulled the picture out of the stack. "No, but there is a New Age store a few doors down that does."

I grabbed a purple throw pillow to toss in my prosperity bagua. "I guess that's all for today."

He started wrapping up my purchases, and I watched his long, thick fingers at work. I cleared my throat. "Can you hang on to the lamp until the other one comes in?" I needed to get another nightstand, too.

He paused and looked at me, narrowing his eyebrows. "You sure you don't want to take it today?"

I shook my head. "I need two in my room." I didn't want to tell him that a single lamp might keep me single.

The corner of his mouth twitched. "You hired Virginia Collins, didn't you?"

I looked down and smiled, tapping my fingers on the glass counter top. "Yes, how did you know?"

His laugh was gorgeous. "Sorry, I shouldn't be so nosy. She sends lots of clients here and I appreciate her business. I'm just surprised someone like you is looking for help with the love bagua." He wrapped my candlesticks with tissue paper while staring at me.

I could feel my cheeks burn. I opened my mouth, and then snapped it shut. I didn't know what to say.

He rubbed the back of his neck. "I'm sorry, I just assumed someone like you would have a boyfriend. Just ignore me. I always say the wrong thing. What do they call it, Foot-In-Mouth disease?"

No, please keep talking. "Do you think it works? Feng shui?"

He squatted behind the counter, searching for a box. "I don't want to insult one of Virginia's clients. That's her thing and she believes it."

Wait, back up the horse. I put my hands on my hips. "But you don't?"

He stood up, crossed his arms and looked at me. "And why are you so quick to believe it does?"

I want to believe it – need to believe it. I lifted one shoulder. "What's the harm?"

"Could be wasting your time and money."

I raised an eyebrow. "At your shop."

"Good point." Again with that grin. He handed me a bag with my candleholders and pillow, and picked up my picture. "Let me carry this to your car."

He pushed the door open with his hip and I followed him out into the warm summer day. "Have you ever heard back from any of Virginia's clients whether or not her techniques work?" I asked. He had me worried now.

He loaded the picture into the back of my Rav-4. "I haven't been invited to any customers' weddings. Not yet anyway." Brushing off his hands, he smiled. "But who knows? No one ever came back for a follow up."

I turned to him. "You must think this is silly."

"I think it makes as much as sense as tossing a penny in a fountain and making a wish." He shrugged and pushed his hands in his pockets.

I slammed my car door, embarrassed that he thought I was foolish. *He's not my type anyway.* "Thanks for your help."

"I'll call you when the lamp comes in so you can take them both home," he said, rubbing his chin.

Was that just to cover a smirk? I jutted my hip to the side and planted my fist there. "And I'll call you when I get my first date. Because this is going to work. Don't worry. I'll follow up."

He smiled at me. "Please do. You can be my first customer to let me know exactly how well this turns out for you."

I hopped in the car and glanced back at him in my rear view mirror as I pulled away. I only wished I felt as confident as I sounded. Maybe this really was just bunk.

I landed a new client over the next few days and found twenty bucks on the sidewalk, so the purple items in my prosperity area seemed to be making a difference, but there was not one call from a guy and no new prospects. Not even one cute barista or sales clerk to flirt with. *Be patient, you haven't implemented all of Virginia's advice,* I reminded myself.

"Brianna?" a male voice asked over the phone when I answered Saturday afternoon. He sounded familiar.

"Yes, this is Brianna Keller." My heart quickened like I was back in eighth grade waiting for Tony Malone to call. He never did, of course.

"It's Zach Michaels, from Interior Inspirations. Your lamp is in."

My heart fell. Somehow I imagined it might be some mysterious man drawn to me through my feng shui changes. Nope. It was the one who thought I was a loon for trying it. "Great. I'll pick it up tonight."

I walked into Interior Inspirations and immediately felt calmed by the music and the great smell—and the great view of the man behind the counter. Mr. Doubting Thomas.

"Are you here to gloat about your string of dates that have magically appeared?" His hair hung past his shoulders, and I tried to decide if it looked even better this way than it had in the ponytail.

I propped my elbows on the counter. "Nope, no date so far."

"Well, you haven't tried the lamps yet. Maybe that's the key." He was holding back a laugh; I just knew it.

"You're probably right."

He set my lamp on the counter. "Do you have anything else on that list of yours?"

I dug through the lipsticks and clutter in my purse and pulled out my crumpled sheet of notes. "Just some amethyst and rose quartz I need to get from the store down the street. And some heart-shaped throw pillows. Do you have any of those?"

He typed the information into his laptop. "Nope. But I can order a few pillows and have them in next week. Can you wait until then?"

No! I want love, now. "Sure. I guess I'll just take the two lamps today."

He closed his cash register drawer. "I'm closing up early tonight. I'll show you that New Age store if you'd like."

I shrugged. "You're very accommodating for a cause you don't believe in."

"Hey, if you're going to try it, I wanna help

you go all out."

We set my lamps in my truck and walked down Main Street. The night was warm, and the sun was starting to slide down the sky.

"How long have you owned your store?" I asked.

"Four years. It was a struggle the first three, but this year I'm finally starting to turn things around."

"Put some purple in your money bagua and it could really take off."

Shaking his head, he laughed. "You will never catch me doing anything like that, I promise."

He stopped in front of a store called Moon Child, with a big moon painted in the window. "Here we are. They should have everything you need."

"Thanks." I was reluctant to see him leave, and I lingered in front of the door.

He shoved his hands in his pockets. "I could help you find the things on your list. Like I said, I've helped lots of Virginia's clients."

"Sure. Yeah, that would be great." I should have just clapped and jumped up and down with a pair of pom-poms.

We stepped inside and I expected a woman in flowing robes to come out and greet us with an offer to read our palms. But a pretty young woman with long dark hair and ripped jeans emerged from the back. Her eyes brightened when she saw Zach.

"Hey Zach, haven't seen you in a while. How's business?"

"Hi, Sherry. It's holding up. You know, despite the economy, it's not bad."

Sherry pouted. "Things have been really slow for me."

"Well, good news," Zach said. "My friend Brianna has quite a few things to buy."

Sherry patted the counter. "Come chat with me while she browses." Her rosy cheeks glowed and her dark hair made her pale blue eyes gleam. She had the batting the eyelashes thing down pat.

I felt my teeth grinding.

He looked back and forth between the two of us. "I'd love to, but I promised Brianna I'd help her find what she needs. She's one of Virginia Collins' clients."

Sherry narrowed her eyes at me and raised her chin. "I'll be in the storeroom if you need me."

Zach set his hand on the small of my back and steered me in the direction of a display in the rear of the store. A big bare tree branch strung with lights was mounted to the wall, while bins of gems and crystals glittered beneath it.

Zach picked up a pink rock and set in his palm. "Pink quartz. The love stone."

I gave him a questioning look. "So, you know about the properties of gems and crystals?"

He dropped the rock back in the bin. "Sure, that doesn't mean I believe them."

I held up a dark blue stone. "What about this one?"

He took it from me and held it toward the light. "That's lapis. Associated with marital love and fidelity."

I snatched it from him. "Better keep one

handy just in case."

I checked out racks of jewelry and flipped through books. I spent at least half an hour browsing around, picking out some interesting essential oils and handmade soaps. I turned to Zach. "You know, you're my first."

"Excuse me?"

I tossed my hair over my shoulders. "I've never been shopping with a man before. And it didn't hurt a bit."

Shaking his head, he chuckled. "I guess when you own your own store, it's not a big deal. It's not like you're looking for clothes. I don't understand why some women need dozens of shoes. Or more than a few pair of jeans."

"Yeah, that's weird." I wasn't opening that jar of worms.

I took my crystals and gems to the counter, where Sherry was rearranging a display of earrings. "Oh, and can I have that hunk of Amethyst on the shelf behind you?" I asked.

"Certainly." Sherry was short with me as I paid for my things. I hoped she hadn't slipped me an unlucky-in-love crystal or some evil charm. I'd have to double-check my things when I got home. I didn't know much about vibes or auras, but something green and jealous was emanating off her.

She babbled some flirty nonsense with Zach, and then he walked me back to my car.

"Can I use your bathroom in the shop?"

"Sure." He unlocked the door, and I dashed to the bathroom—even though I didn't have to go. Then, while he was occupied with something

behind the register, I hid the hunk of purple
Amethyst in the back left corner of his shop,
behind a big trunk. I snatched a purple napkin
from a nearby table display and tucked that
behind the trunk, too. That was his wealth bagua,
and I wanted to do a little experiment.

I surprised the girls by showing up for brunch
at the Parkside Bistro Sunday morning.
"Brianna! It's so nice to see you. That
handsome gentleman from the wedding called
Mildred," Patsy said. "They went out last night
on their fourth date."
I pulled up a chair. "Tell me everything," I
said.
We giggled and chatted over mimosas and
crepes and I finally learned their names.
"What about you? Have you met anyone?"
Mildred asked. She'd been the one in the lavender
dress. "Are Virginia's methods helping you yet?"
I frowned and shook my head.
Ettie, minus her rhinestone purse, patted my
hand. "These things can take time."
"I promise you things will change," Virginia
said.
"I've got another wedding to go to next
weekend. We'll see."

This time, I tried dress number two, the
strapless, pale, pink sheath Sarah loved on me.
And this time there were single guys right at my
table—one seated right next to me with
horrendous breath, another across from me who
never asked one question about me, and the one

who asked if he could have the rest of my steak since I wasn't going to finish it. This time, I didn't even wait around for the cake.

Zach had left a message that my pillows were in. I stopped by after work and I knew he'd ask how things were going in the romance department.

The bells on the door jingled and a smile unfurled when he saw me. "I'm surprised you have time to squeeze me in with all the dates you must be lining up."

I picked up a stained glass bowl and pretended to inspect it. "Maybe I'm just too picky. There was a very nice fellow I met at a wedding this weekend with a gorgeous toupee who was just dying to take me to bingo." I set down the bowl and looked at him.

"I stand corrected; it is working." He winked at me.

I turned away from him so he couldn't see my blush. I blushed easier than a bee made honey. "Wow, who cleared out your shop?" I looked back at him and he shrugged.

"It's been crazy busy around here. Stuff that hasn't moved in months is going left and right." He snapped his fingers. "And all without feng shui. Imagine that."

It was hard to hide my smile. I was dying to drag him over to the chest and show him the hunk of amethyst I'd hidden. But why did he see such quick results and not me?

He looked at his watch. "I close at seven on Tuesdays. Wanna grab a drink? There's a new pub down the street I want to check out, the Sundowner. I like to support the locals when I can. And I have a brand new catalog you might want to look through."

Hmm, does he want my company or my business?
"That would be great."

We ordered a bottle of wine and a plate of cheese and fruit. Our fingers brushed as we both reached for the same slice of smoked Gouda.

He pulled his hand back and fiddled with his silverware. "So you're not into Bingo, huh?"

"Hard to believe, I know."

One corner of his mouth quirked up. "Helpful information, I'll be sure to make note of it."

Well, if that wasn't an invitation to do a little flirting of my own, I don't know what was. "Enough about the search for my missing love life, how is it you don't have a girlfriend, Zach?"

He laughed and set down his wine. "I hate to use the work excuse, but launching a new business takes more time than I ever imagined. And I do all the support work myself—the bookkeeping, marketing and all that. I'm lucky I get to spend any quality time with my dog. And all I get from her is an occasional lick on the cheek."

I fingered the stem of my glass. "It seems to me Miss Moon Child would be interested."

"Sherry?" He shook his head. "No, she's not interested. We're just friends."

My jaw dropped. "You're seriously telling me you don't think she's into you?"

He looked at me like I was speaking Mandarin Chinese while he was holding a Spanish dictionary.

I reached over and patted his hand. "Zach, my poor boy. Not only were you born with Foot-in-Mouth disease, but you seem to also be lacking proper flirting radar."

He scrunched his eyebrows and poured more wine. "That's not true."

"When we're done here, let's go to her place and tell me you don't think she's hot for you." It was a little strange to be steering Zach toward Sherry when sparks were starting to pop between us, but he really wasn't my type. He was so different from any other guy I'd dated, I was certain it wouldn't work.

"Well, it doesn't really matter, because I'm not interested in her." He finished off a slice of cheese.

"Chicken."

"What's the point?"

I snapped an apple wedge and pointed it at him. "I think it's important that you know your flirting radar is shot. Knowing there's a problem is the first step to recovery."

"Just so long as you don't try to fix it with rocks or crystals."

We finished the wine and cheese, and he led me down to her store, very determined to prove me wrong.

Sherry's eyes brightened when he walked in. She set down her magazine and came straight over, smoothing her hands down her hips while nibbling her bottom lip. Then she saw me.

"You're here helping your customer again?"

"No. Well, yes. We were out for a drink, and

Brianna said she needed to stop in for a few more things."

Frowning, she looked away. "Out for a drink?"

"Yeah, I wanted to check out the new pub. Have you been?"

She shook her head. "Stop by some night after work, and we can go together." She clenched her hands together in front of her, which pushed her cleavage out. I wouldn't have been surprised if she hiked up her skirt.

I smirked and wandered back to the crystal bin, just to make it look like I really did need to pick something up. I grabbed a few more pieces of pink quartz. Maybe the ones I'd bought were duds. I took them up to the register and she rang me out—while talking to Zach the entire time.

We left the store, and a pouting Sherry. "See?" I said.

"What? We're friends. We were talking."

I rolled my eyes. "No wonder you're single." I jerked my thumb over my shoulder. "If you're in, she's in. Trust me." Surprisingly, I felt a little jab to the gut saying that.

He shook his head. "I'm still not convinced. But even so, it doesn't matter."

I pulled out a hunk of quartz. "Apparently, you need this more than I do."

He stepped back and held up his hands like it might bite him.

I laughed and moved forward until his back was pressed against the brick building. I held up the rock between us like a shiny little prize.

He stared at me with those eyes, and I felt a

flush down to my toes.

"Just what do you intend to do with that?" he asked, in a husky voice.

"The question is what are you going to do with it?" I tucked it in his front pocket and he sucked in a breath. "Give it a shot," I said.

"With Sherry? No."

I swallowed hard and he stepped closer to me. He reached for my hand and we stared at each other, with our fingers linked. There was definitely something there. But he quickly drew back his hand and smoothed his hair. "There are a few things I forgot to do. In there." He pointed to his door. "I'll see you soon, Brianna."

He walked into the store, and I didn't dare follow. We were both surprised by that hot touch of skin. I'd always thought he was nice eye-candy, but now I was imagining maybe he could be more than that.

And I kept thinking about it the rest of the week. Sarah and I hit a new place for lunch every day, hoping we might find some single guys doing the same. But any time I saw anyone who might be a possibility, I thought about Zach, with his easy smile and his intense eyes and how his fingers might feel on the rest of me. He was a far cry from Mr. Clean Cut and Corporate who was my current "ideal." Maybe my ideal was all wrong.

Friday night, the only thing I wanted to do was see him again and find out if there was really a spark or not. I was going to another wedding the next night, and this time it wouldn't be so bad if I didn't meet anyone. Not with Zach keeping me preoccupied. I parked on Main Street down from his shop and double-checked my hair and makeup in the rearview mirror. My hair was now more magenta than red and I was feeling sassy. Everything was looking good, so I sauntered over to his door and went in just before closing time.

His smile made it worth the trip. "Hey, how are you?" He looked me up and down. "More colorful, that's for sure. I like it."

I curled a piece of hair around my finger. "Thanks."

"Was that one of Virginia's feng shui things?"

I laughed. "No. Changing my hair color is a hobby of mine." I walked over to a new chair he had on display, sat down and crossed my legs. "Comfy." I patted the armrests. "Business still booming?"

He pulled a chair next to me and sat down. "Yeah, it is."

My instincts were telling me to wait until I confessed about my secret feng shui treatment. "Great."

He reached over and set his hand next to mine. "I had fun with you the other night. Do you have plans tonight? Or are the eligible men finally rolling in?"

I gave him a slow smile, pleased by his attention. "One possibility. But no one else." I didn't get it; why was his business booming while my love life was a bust? Besides Zach, there was no one. The damn feng shui was working for him and he didn't he believe in it!

"I don't have any plans tonight. Other than

coming here to see you."

"Wanna hit the pub again?" He walked over to his front door and flipped the sign from open to closed and pulled down the shade. He turned back to me and the look he gave me hit me straight in the gut.

Oh, yeah. There's a spark. I took that as my cue and walked over to him, cutting the space between us to just inches. "Maybe I don't want to go to the pub."

He raised one eyebrow and smiled. "What are you thinking instead?"

I pressed my hand against his chest. "I'm wondering if that's a piece of rose quartz in your pocket, or if you're just happy to see me?" I wasn't too bad at flirting once I found a worthy subject. And that was always my problem.

He looked down and his hair swung in his face, obscuring what might have been a blush. He tucked his hand in jeans pocket and pulled out the rock. "I like it. It feels lucky." He set it on the counter and wrapped one hand around the small of my back.

I tipped my head up to look at him. "I guess it is." His lips covered mine and he cupped the back of my head with his hand.

His kiss was soft, but demanding, then he broke away. "Hang on one minute." Holding up a finger, he dashed to the door. He flicked off the lights and grabbed a candle and a box of long matches.

"Get two candles!" I called. "One's unlucky."

He laughed and shook his head, but he

grabbed another candle and set them on the counter. He lit each one, then grabbed a few big pillows and tossed them on the floor. Taking my hand again, he pulled me down to sit on the cushy seating arrangement.

"I like this even better than the pub."

"One more minute." He disappeared to a room behind the counter, and emerged with a bottle of champagne and two glasses. "Leftover from my holiday open house last year." He popped the bottle and poured us each a glass.

He sat down next to me and I leaned against him. His shirt was soft, yet his shoulder was hard against my cheek. I took a sip of the sweet, bubbly liquid and I looked up at him. Taking my face in his hands, he kissed me. Gently at first, then more urgent.

I tangled my hands through his hair, and he lowered me onto the pillows. His eyes swept over me and he smiled. "Yeah, much better than the pub."

We lay next to each other, talking and laughing, in between some very hot kisses. He wasn't any more forward than that, and it felt like a sweet first date back in high school.

"I have a confession to make," I told him.

"That usually leads to bad news."

He sat up and I followed. "No, not at all. Remember you said your sales spiked for no reason?" I wrapped my arms around my knees.

"Yeah, and I'm still busy."

I wrinkled my nose. "Well, I might have done a few things in your wealth bagua."

He narrowed one eye. "Come again?"

"Feng shui. I added some purple to the section of your store that correlates with wealth. And your sales took off."

"What did you do?"

"Come see." I reached out for his hand and led him to the trunk where I had hidden the Amethyst and the purple napkin.

He picked up the silky fabric and rubbed it with his fingers, laughing. "I can't say for sure that's what did it, but I'll leave it right where it is."

"That's not enough to convince you?"

He shrugged. "It's probably just coincidence."

"And the pink quartz I gave you hasn't helped in the love department?" I gave him a little punch in the chest.

He kissed my nose. "I've been planning to kiss you since I first saw you, so no. The pink quartz had no effect."

I set my forehead against his. "Why won't you believe?" I liked the idea of being in control of my love life for once, and feng shui would give me that control. If it worked, that is.

"I want to know why you *do* believe?" He kissed away my frown.

I looked at him. "I want it to work. So I have to believe."

"Well, here's something to believe. I want to see you again. Can we get together next week?" His lips were still inches from mine.

Not wanting to throw myself at the man, I said, "I'll stop by during lunch and we can make plans."

After another kiss, I floated home and

wondered if he could be honest to goodness boyfriend material. Maybe the feng shui stuff was finally working for me.

"Where's Charles?" my mother asked as we sat down at the reception. No, not the single girls' table this time, this was even worse—I was parked next to my mother.

"I told you it would be hard for him to get the night off." I sighed and figured I'd throw her a bone. "But maybe you're right."

She perked up at that. "About what?" That's not a phrase she heard very often from me.

"About Charles. I don't think it's going to work out. I hardly ever see him. Sometimes it feels like we're not even dating." *Ain't that the truth...*

She patted my hand. "Yesterday, I was asking the technician giving me my mammogram if she knew any single men."

I dropped my head in my hands and squeezed my eyes tight like she might disappear. "No, you didn't."

She nodded, quite proud of herself. "I did. And her next-door neighbor's sister has a fabulous son who just got divorced. He's a lawyer."

"Yes, that sounds really, really fabulous. I'll be fine mom. Just trust me."

To humor her, I danced with several men who only reaffirmed for me what a catch Zach would be.

I brought a picnic basket to his shop on Tuesday and joined him behind the counter for lunch. He loved sweets as much as I did and didn't touch red meat, I learned. I got a seriously hot kiss before leaving, and we made plans to go out Friday night. I was liking this guy more and more each day.

Surprising Zach with an unexpected visit right before closing the next night seemed like a perfect, flirty thing to do. I bought a big slice of praline cheesecake from a bakery a few shops down from his, grabbed two forks and headed for his store. I couldn't turn down my smile thinking about seeing him again.

I walked past the Moon Child shop and froze; Zach was inside with Sherry. His back was to me, but her head was on his shoulder and her arms were wrapped around his neck. They looked very much like he and I had looked the other night. Then he dipped his mouth to her ear.

My chest tightened and I swore. I tossed the cheesecake in a nearby garbage can. I stalked back to my car, wondering if I'd ever thrown out dessert before.

I went home and shoved all the heart-shaped pillows in my closet. This whole idea had been stupid. Not only was I not finding love, I was managing to get my heart broken by the first interesting guy I'd met in a long time. Maybe Sherry did give me some bad love charms, I thought. *No she didn't, because none of this nonsense is real.* It was stupid and I never should have tried it.

The next day, I gathered up the candleholders and candles I hadn't really used. Maybe Zach would give me some cash back for them. I wasn't wasting my time or money on this—or him—anymore.

He greeted me with his killer smile, but I didn't return the favor. "Everything alright?" he asked.

"You win. You were right. This nonsense doesn't work, and I was wondering if I could return some of this stuff for partial credit. Or just take it back. I don't care. I don't want to see it in my house. And cancel the order for the pillows." I'd asked for two more heart pillows to scatter around the apartment, that's how desperate I'd become. Stupid, is more like it.

He stepped from behind the counter and folded his hand around my elbow. "Brianna, you can't get discouraged like this. I know you've met some winners the past few weeks, but I thought we had a nice time the other night. Don't I count? I really like spending time with you."

And how many other women? I didn't play that game. "It seemed like it, but it's just not right for me." I couldn't have meant that much to him if he was hooking up with Sherry a few days later.

He crossed his arms. "I'm sorry to hear that. I thought maybe…"

I shook my head. "Thanks for your help, Zach." I left his store with no intention of ever coming back to Interior Inspirations.

I called Virginia to cancel her follow-up appointment that weekend, but she insisted on coming. I didn't want to hurt her feelings, so I agreed to let her come.

"This isn't working," I told her when she

showed up on Saturday. I wasn't going to tell her what had happened with Zach. It was too mortifying.

"It's not like ordering takeout, dear. Give it time." She bent down to look under my bed. "And clear out under here. You shouldn't have anything under your bed. It's the most important piece of furniture in your life and the energy needs to flow all around it." She waved her hands in a swooping motion to make her point, but I wasn't buying it.

I frowned, but followed along as she inspected the rest of my place.

"You've done good work. Now just get on with the business of living your life and see the changes that come to you."

I crossed my arms. I didn't want to insult her and tell her I didn't believe in this anymore.

She poked a finger in my chest. "And change your attitude. You need to be open to the idea of love. It's not just going to break down the door and find you."

I opened the door to let her out, and there was Zach, holding a package for me.

She looked back and forth between us and shrugged. "Or maybe it will," she said slyly.

"Hello, Virginia," Zach said

"I wasn't aware you made deliveries, Zach," she said.

"Yes, well..." he mumbled.

"Brianna, I'll see you in two weeks." She winked at me and left.

Zach turned to me. "Your pillows came in. I thought I'd drop them off."

I turned from him and led him inside. "I cancelled the order, remember?"

"But I want you to have them. They're on me. I don't want you to give up on love. Just give it a chance."

I crossed my arms and blinked back the sadness creeping over me. "You were right. It was a silly idea. I'm just humoring Virginia because I like her."

"Beautiful and considerate. Quite the catch. That's why I'm not willing to give up."

I ignored him. "Been busy this week?" I shouldn't sound so jealous. It's not like we were officially dating. But I could've sworn there had been real passion behind his kisses.

"Yeah, I have been busy. It's been a horrible week. Sherry's shop got flooded. Water pipe burst and I've been helping her clean up. She's close to losing everything." He shook his head. "She was despondent. I tried my best to comfort her, but she just hung on to me and cried. I didn't know what the hell to do."

"When was this?"

"Tuesday."

"Oh." The lump in my stomach was going away. Most Likely to Jump To Conclusions had blown it again. I felt bad for her loss, but I hated how much she must have loved being in his arms. She was probably going to try to strike while the sympathy iron was hot, trying to move his kindness on to something more.

My heart clenched. I knew Sherry wanted Zach; and that's when I realized I did, too. I really did. And I had more weapons to use in this fight than just my new feng shui adjustments. I pointed to the pillows he was holding. "Can you bring those into my bedroom for me?"

"Oh, of course." He followed me with the bag and set it down on my bed.

Luckily, Virginia had lit candles in my room and showed me how to stage my bed with pillows on both sides, so it suggested two people shared it. I'm glad I hadn't told her not to bother. "What do you think?" I asked him.

He ran his hand down the back of his head. "It's really nice. Very inviting. I think it's going to definitely bring love to your life."

I sighed. I hoped I hadn't blown it with him. I took his hand to make myself clear.

He looked down at our hands, and then into my eyes. "I'm confused. I thought you weren't interested. I guess my flirting radar really doesn't work."

I took a deep breath and fessed up. "I saw you with Sherry the other day, hugging her. I thought you two had hooked up, and I got jealous."

He smiled. "You're right. She's interested. But like I said, I'm not."

My heart lodged in my throat and I swallowed hard. I needed a drink. "Can I get you some wine?"

He gazed at our hands intertwined and smiled for a long minute. "No," he said. "I've already had wine with you. I want more of this." He placed a finger under my chin and raised my lips to his. He kissed me in the softest, most passionate way I'd ever been kissed.

I pushed the pillows off the bed and pulled him toward me.

"We're messing up all this feng shui stuff," he whispered in my ear.

I kissed him back. "No, we're just proving it works."

"Confession time," he said.

"Uh oh. That's never good, right?"

He shrugged. "Sometimes it is. Here goes. I've got two pink candles sitting on my dresser." His lips left a trail of kisses across my cheek and over to my ear.

"What? You tried feng shui? At home?"

"Once I saw what those purple things did in the shop I thought it was worth a shot. I figured maybe you weren't getting together with the right guy — like me — because *his* love bagua was off."

"Handsome and open minded. What more could I want?" I laughed.

"What are you doing the rest of the night?" he asked.

I looked over at the evening dress hanging on my closet door. "I was supposed to be going to a wedding, but something suddenly came up."

"And then what happened?" Mildred asked, her forkful of quiche quivering in the air.

I crossed my arms. "Ladies, ladies. I don't kiss and tell." I laughed. "Well, at least not everything."

They started booing, and people at other tables turned to look at the ruckus seven old ladies were causing.

"Fine, fine. We kissed some more." I could

still feel the softness of his lips on mine the next morning as I sat there at brunch.

"I told you," Virginia said. "I told you you'd find love. I just didn't think it would work so quickly."

Ettie frowned. "I think she just met a cute guy cause she was at his store so often. How do you know it was feng shui?"

I popped a grape in my mouth. "I don't care what it was. I like him a lot. I'm keeping those crystals in my bedroom. And I won't dare ever put a single candle in my apartment again. Only pairs for this girl."

Two weeks later, Virginia bustled up to me in the reception hall. "Thanks for your help. So, everything is set? Each guest has two rose quartz crystals as a favor?"

I nodded. "I set them out just like you asked." Along with the meaning of the stones printed on the back of her business card. She was quite the businesswoman. "I think Mildred will be thrilled." I said. She and the silver haired gentlemen she met at Carly's wedding were getting hitched. I glanced around the ballroom. "It's perfect."

Zach came up behind me and wrapped his arms around my waist. "Everything's been perfect since I met you."

I turned to look at him. "Was it the feng shui or fate?" I asked, brushing my lips against his.

He shrugged. "Who knows? Maybe it does matter where you line up your bed and what you've got underneath it, but I think it mostly matters that you find the right place for your heart." He smiled at me. "I know I did."

We kissed, forgetting Virginia and the girls still setting up the tables, and the staff members at the Parkside milling around assembling the reception room.

Finally, I had a date to bring to a wedding. I had a feeling we'd be throwing a reception of our own, soon enough.

I rested my head against his chest, and felt his heart thud against my cheek. "The perfect place for my heart is right next to yours."

"Never Been Dumped"
By Lisa Scott

Her excuse was the same for each guy because it was true, "I'm waiting for a friend." But that didn't stop the parade of men from wandering over to the table in the corner and asking Rachel Miller to dance. Sitting alone listening to the band was an open invitation she didn't realize she was sending. These guys possessed the same radar as an obnoxious dog that always sniffs out the one person in the room who doesn't want to be licked.

She looked down at the long, black wrap-around skirt exposing her thigh and frowned. *That certainly doesn't help.* She tried holding it closed with one hand. Her friends teased her for having zero instincts about men. She never knew when they were really interested, and when she did go out with someone, she always ended up with first date remorse.

The wedding she'd attended the weekend before was the perfect example. Her Great Aunt Mildred had tied the knot, and Rachel had been asked to dance a dozen times at the reception. Lindsey's friend Luke had been there and asked her three times. Her cousin Brianna was there, too, trying to set her up with some of her friends. *Maybe I should bring an ankle brace and fake an injury next time.*

Great Aunt Mildred gave out shiny nuggets of rose quartz crystals as favors. The stones were supposed to bring the guests love; some crazy new age thing. Rachel left those puppies sitting on the

173

table. She didn't want to attract any more love in her life. Right now, she was trying to repel it.

She looked up and spotted another guy smiling at her under a thick red mustache. She snapped away her gaze. Not everyone comes to a bar looking to hook up, she grumbled to herself.

The guys hadn't taken it well. *Am I sitting in a must-dance zone?* She'd been sworn at more than once. But she didn't care. While she was single, she truly wasn't interested. Not even in the George Clooney look alike who had asked if she was certain she didn't want to dance with *him*.

Although she had pondered his offer for a moment, before gathering up her wits again.

She settled her hand on her chin, watching the country western group that Lindsey had wanted to see. It was Friday night, and she'd bet a bundle that Lindsey was still at work with her boss, because being alone in his office — sometimes on the couch, sometimes on his desk — made it all that more exciting.

She was so killing Lindsey.

Half-drunk couples with busy hands cluttered the dance floor, and she pulled out her cell to check the time. Nine forty-five. If Lindsey didn't show by ten, she was leaving.

Another man made his way over. She sighed and looked up at him standing by her table.

His blue eyes locked on hers, and one corner of his mouth curled up. "I'd ask if I could buy you a drink, but you haven't touched the one in front of you. And I'd invite you to dance, but I know you'll say no. So let me ask, why is a woman sitting alone at a bar, not drinking and turning down every guy who comes her way?" He was tall, with dirty blonde hair curling around his ears and might have been her type a few years back.

She swirled the liquid in her glass, but didn't take a drink. "You've been watching."

"You're hard to miss." He gripped the back of the chair in front of him, his fingers tensing around the wooden slat.

She closed her eyes and smiled. "I'm waiting for my friend to show up, but I suspect she's ditching me for a guy. And turns out, I'm not in a drinking mood." The band finished its song and cleared the stage for a break. They promised to be back in ten.

He glanced over his shoulder. "A sea of men will be storming your table now. Why don't I join you and keep them at bay while you wait?"

Now her mouth curled up. "Will that count towards your community service?"

He placed his hand on his heart and jerked back like he'd been punched. "Ouch, now I have to sit down, that hurt."

Biting her lip to stifle a laugh, she shrugged. "Sure, but I'm leaving in fifteen minutes if she doesn't show."

He held out his hand. "Drake Johnson."

His hand was firm and warm when she shook it. Always a good quality in a man—if she'd been looking. "Rachel Miller." She took a sip of her drink, now watered down from the melting ice cubes.

He spun the chair around, straddled it, and sat across from her. "So, why not give some poor guy here a shot and kill time while you wait? Do you have a boyfriend?"

She shook her head.

He shook a finger at her. "Let me guess. Too busy with your career for men?"

"Nope. I've got time, or I wouldn't be sitting here waiting for a friend." Her freelance graphic design business meant she could make her own hours. Just one of the reasons she loved it.

He narrowed his eyes. "An arranged marriage looming?"

She laughed. "That might be easier than the dating scene."

"Ahh. You're coming off a nasty breakup and you're not ready to have your heart broken again." He crossed his arms and looked very satisfied.

She blew out a breath. "Nasty breakup, yes. But a broken heart? No. I wish."

He cocked his head, looking confused. "You wish your heart was broken? What, you need an excuse for a weekend long chocolate binge?" He planted his elbows on the table and leaned forward.

"It's too ridiculous to explain. Trust me." She held up her hand like she might be able to keep this hot guy and his personal questions from getting any closer.

"Now you have to explain. I love ridiculous."

She nibbled on her lower lip, wondering how to tell him this without sounding like a total bitch. *Who cares? You'll never see him again.* "I'm sick of breaking hearts." She looked at him, waiting for his reaction.

He slapped his hand over his own heart.

"Wow."

"No, seriously. It's really hard to break up with someone who still likes you. I'm always the one who ends it, and I hate disappointing them. It sucks, and I'm no good at it."

"Sucks more than getting dumped?"

One shoulder jerked up. "I don't know. I've never been dumped."

He stared at her, like he was waiting her to fess up the truth. "Oh, come on. Everyone's been dumped. In high school, getting dumped was a sport for me." He jerked his thumb against his chest. "I majored in getting dumped in college."

She leaned back in her chair. "Sounds like you have a lot to offer the ladies."

"Hilarious. So you're telling me no man has ever broken up with you? Not once in your life?"

She shook her head. "It's true. And I'm sick of the phone calls afterward. Sad at first, then desperate, then angry." She took another drink. "I once had to get a restraining order on a guy who just wouldn't take no for an answer. That's why I'm done with dating for a long time." Her hand sliced the air. "So, why bother dancing with a guy when there's no chance it will go anywhere? At least I'm not leading them on. You'd think I'd get credit for that."

"I'll dump you," he offered.

She laughed. "Best offer I've had all night."

He moved to the chair next to her and they were elbow to elbow. "No, seriously. I'm in town for the summer. I'm leaving August 31st. Let's go out until then, and I promise to dump you. I don't do long distance relationships."

177

"Why not?"

"That's a long story I'll tell you a few weeks into our relationship on some warm summer night when we're getting cozy under the stars."

She giggled. "Again, ridiculous."

"Like I said, I'm all about ridiculous."

"What if you change your mind and stay? Then I'll have to dump you. Defeats the whole purpose."

"Absolutely not. I start culinary school in the fall, and I'm not giving that up. And no way do I want to have a relationship distracting me while I'm in school."

She tipped her head and stared at him. His dimples seemed permanently carved in his cheeks, with that ever-present smile. His hair curled around his face in a boyish way that probably got him out of a lot of trouble. Irresistible was a word that came to mind. "What if I get so annoyed with you before that, that I have no choice but to dump you? Seems like a good possibility."

"Won't happen. I'm a good kisser."

"And incredibly cocky." She gave him a playful nudge and was pleased to find he had a muscular arm.

"Play to your strengths."

Rachel was intrigued, but it was a stupid idea; the kind that could only be concocted at a bar. Crossing her arms, she gave him the bad news. "Sorry. I guess I'll always have to wonder about your prowess."

He gave her a playful pout. "You sure? I've dumped plenty girls in my life. Made a few cry even. I'd be brilliant. You'd need gallons of ice cream to get over me."

She laughed. "I'm quite sure, but thanks for the offer."

He stood up. "It was worth a shot."

"Good luck with culinary school."

He looked back as he walked away. "Good luck finding a guy to dump you. Can't imagine anyone would want to."

She pushed away her unfinished drink and reached for her car keys in her purse. She grabbed her cell to text Lindsey that she was leaving, but Lindsey had beaten her to it. *Tyler and I are officially a couple! Call you tomorrow.*

Ugh. If Tyler and Lindsey were dating—and not just sleeping together—she'd certainly be stepping up the campaign to get Rachel to go out with Tyler's best friend Luke—Mr. Persistent from the wedding. "He's got the wonderful accent," Lindsey had scolded, as if that were reason enough to give him a whirl. "And he's rich!" Lindsey was full of ideas for the two of them; and Luke was just full of himself. That added up to bad news.

She rubbed her temples and looked up, and saw another man standing in front of her. "Wanna dance, sugar?"

"No, thanks." She gave him a feeble smile.

He hitched up his jeans. "You think you're too good for us here? You been turning down men all night." He looked her up and down. "You some kind of city slicker?"

Just because I'm not wearing cowboy boots? Why couldn't she just lie and say she had a boyfriend? But Rachel didn't like to lie, even if it made things easier. It was some residual Catholic schoolgirl thing. She twisted her lips. Having a boyfriend would make things a lot easier. She'd be able to fend off Luke, at least. And she certainly had some time on her hands now that Lindsey was going to be busy with Rob. Plus, Drake was hot. And funny. If she were the one-night stand type, he'd fit the bill.

But this is more like a two-month stand.

She looked over at Drake with his back against the bar, watching her. He raised an eyebrow and smiled. She pointed at him. "That's my boyfriend. He doesn't really appreciate me dancing with other men."

The guy wandered away, and she crooked her finger at Drake to come over.

He bumped into a chair as he dashed over to her. "A change of heart?"

"Not if you're going to be obnoxious about it."

He crossed his arms. "So we *are* going to go out. Hot damn."

"Let's leave."

"Ready to try out my kissing already?" He patted his pockets. "Where did I put that chapstick?"

She stood up with a sigh and slung her purse over her shoulder. "No, I'm just ready to call it a night and I told that guy you're my boyfriend. Plus, I'm not sure how you'd hold up in a bar fight, so we better leave."

"Not well. I'm a lover not a fighter."

"Let's just go."

He moved closer behind her and put his hands on her shoulders. "Whatever my honey bunny wants."

She wiggled her shoulders away from him. "Absolutely not. No pet names."

"Of course, pumpkin."

She glared at him and headed for the door.

"Kidding," he said, catching up to her. "Wait. Let me walk you to your car. My realtor got jumped in a parking lot last summer. Gotta be careful."

She paused, and he held the door when they stepped out into the warm night.

"Thank you," she said. "Although, leaving with a stranger might not be the safest thing either."

"I'm not a stranger. I'm your new boyfriend. The one with a scheduled departure date who just saved you from a horde of men." He reached for her hand, and she stepped away.

"Slow down, we haven't even had our first date yet."

"No goodnight kiss?" he teased. His pale blue eyes practically glowed under the lights in the parking lot and the effect shot straight to her knees.

She shook it off and looked up at the full moon in the sky. "Please don't make me dump you already."

He slid his hands in his pockets. "Okay, how about dinner tomorrow?"

"That sounds perfect."

He programmed her number into his phone and walked her to her car. Leaning in her open window, he grinned. "Good night, sweet cheeks."

She rolled up the window on him, and he

watched her pull away.

Rachel drove home wondering how she had made such a stupid agreement without having even finished one drink. When Lindsey finally came up to breathe from her new relationship, she was totally blaming this on her.

She shouldn't have been nervous for their dinner date, but she was. Probably because she was worried it would be bad — atrocious. Then what? She really wanted to have one relationship where she wasn't the one who walked away.

Slipping on a silky pink sundress with matching shoes, she told herself to lighten up and have fun. This was a relationship with an expiration date. She might be revolutionizing the whole dating scene, like car rentals did for the automobile industry. She perked up at that thought.

Drake showed up right at six with a bunch of roses the exact color of her dress. She hadn't been expecting that. "Thanks," she said, quickly transferring them to a vase in the kitchen, hoping her cheeks weren't turning pink, too.

"Cute place," he said, strolling through her apartment. He picked up a throw pillow from her couch, fluffed it, and tossed it back. "Will I be getting my own shelf in the medicine cabinet?" The tips of his hair were still wet from a shower. A subtle smell of musk and spice hit her.

She sucked in her breath. "How do you know I'm not going to back out on this deal and dump you before the week is over?"

Her kitty, Hijinx, crept out from under the

couch and wound himself between Drake's feet. Hijinx usually didn't slink out to investigate until the third or fourth date.

Drake reached down to scratch his ears, which earned an enthusiastic head butt from the cat. "You won't bail, because you seem like the kind of her girl who sticks to her promises." He stood up and clapped his hands together. "So, shall we skip dinner and spend the night making out?"

She dropped her head back and closed her eyes.

"Just throwing it out there in case you wanted to speed things along. No worries. Since I suspected you might be hungrier for food than a taste of my lips, I made reservations for Italian, Thai, and gourmet burgers. Take your pick."

Thorough and thoughtful. That scored a couple of points to counterbalance the cockiness. "Let's do Thai."

Drake did everything right. He opened her car door, let her choose the radio station in the car, and pulled out her chair. She hadn't found a reason to ding him any points so far. It was like he'd flipped on his good behavior switch. Things would be so much easier if men came equipped with one of *those*.

"Nice place," she said. Bright tapestries covered the walls and crystal chandeliers hung from the ceiling. Soft Zen music played overhead. It was casual but elegant, and surprisingly, she was looking forward to their evening together.

They ordered four dishes to split and didn't have any difficulty choosing ones they both liked.

"What do you do for a living?" he asked while they waited for their food to arrive.

"I'm a freelance graphic artist. I've got an awesome boss." She jabbed her thumb against her chest. "Me. And how about you?"

He held out one hand and started listing past occupations with the flick of each finger. "I've been a lifeguard, a telemarketer, a dog walker, and a limo driver. I'm unemployed for the moment while I wait to go to culinary school. I'm hoping this is the career that sticks."

That would have set off warning bells on any other first date. Flaky and unemployed usually weren't the best qualities in a man. But this time, it didn't matter. "Why are you in Springfield this summer instead of home?"

"I'm staying in my Grandmother's house while the family tries to sell it. Everyone else lives out of town. She died last year and we haven't been able to sell the house."

She set down her fork. "I'm sorry. You must miss her."

"Thanks. We were really close. Grandma was really the only one in my family who 'got' me. She encouraged me to pursue all my interests, didn't give me shit when I dropped out of fencing class after six months—after announcing I'd make it to the Olympics some day. She liked that I tried different things, even though other people in the family wondered when I was going to get my shit together. Funny thing is, she never had a job, and never left this town, but she could still appreciate a dreamer like me."

"Culinary school, huh?"

184

"Yep. Back in Philadelphia. Grandma and I liked to cook together. She said I was a natural, so I'm going to give that a shot."

Rachel mentally removed the label flighty and replaced it with risk taker. "You're lucky. My parents practically wanted a signed contract of my career intentions before I graduated high school.

"You knew that's what you wanted to do? Graphic art?"

I nodded. "My life has been filled with few surprises."

"I'm the ying to your yang. That's what my grandma always said about me and her."

She took another big helping of Pad Thai. "What's it like living in her house without her there?"

"Sounds weird, but I keep expecting her to walk into the room. Like she's in the kitchen, just finishing up dinner."

She took a long drink of her smoky Thai iced tea. "I didn't know my grandparents. They were all gone before I was born. My parents had me when they were older."

"Only child?"

"Yep. My father died a few years back and mom remarried." She looked down, trying to push away the sad feelings.

He reached over and squeezed her hand without saying a word.

She surprised herself by squeezing back. But then again, there was no chance he'd get the wrong idea by the gesture.

They chatted and shared stories until the rest of the diners had cleared out. When their waiter tidied up the tables around them for the second time, Rachel said, "I think it's time to go." *And then what?*

Her heart thumped in her chest on the way home, and she realized she was actually nervous. When was the last time a date ended with her feeling nervous instead of annoyed?

*****

Damn, he wanted to kiss her. Like, an into-the-next-morning kiss. But he wasn't getting the same vibes in return on the car ride home. She'd laugh and then pull back; smile, then gaze out the window. They both knew this was going to end. They could mark it on their calendars if they wanted. So what was behind her caution? Dinner had gone better than expected. He'd felt a connection; now he felt her hesitation.

She was quiet for much of the ride back to her place. Possibly playing out what would happen when they got there? Was she regretting their arrangement?

Well, he wasn't going to rush this. She probably expected him to be all over her. If he were going to do anything with their two months together, he'd prove to her she didn't know everything about men. And when he did kiss her, he'd enjoy every second of it. He'd make sure she did, too.

They pulled into the parking lot in front of her apartment building and he hopped out of the car, opened her door, and walked her to the front step. He grabbed her hand. "I think that went quite well for a first date." He thought about joking that they had plenty of leftovers for the morning, but she was probably expecting that.

"Yes, the food was great. And so was the company." She looked up at him and her amber eyes framed by the honey-blonde hair almost buckled his knees.

He took a deep breath and squeezed her hand. "I'll call you tomorrow. But remember I'm not working and I've got a lot of time on my hands. Be sure to let me know when to back off." He winked. "Don't want you to dump me."

She blinked at him. "Okay. Do you want to come in? Have a drink?"

Did he? Like mad. But he wanted to be sure she really, truly wanted him when they shared their first kiss. Some might call it calculating, but he just figured it was caution. "Let's just enjoy tonight. I'll call tomorrow, and we'll plan our next date."

She took a step back from him and let out a laugh. Then she shook her head and took out her keys. "Thanks, Drake. That was fun. And unexpected."

"Don't be so sure you always know how things are going to work out, Rachel."

She looked back at him before walking through her door.

He trudged back to his car. Yeah, driving home from that face — that body — sucked. Big time. But like his grandmother's beef stew, some things needed to simmer for a while.

He flicked on the front hall light in his Grandmother's big old Victorian house. How old was that chandelier in the front hall, anyway? He looked up at it, wondering what lucky family would be living here. Not that he wanted strangers taking over this place. This home had been the soul of their family. How many holidays had they celebrated here back when most of the family still lived in town? The huge mahogany table in the dining room seated twelve. But even that wasn't enough room for their clan. The kids crowded round the kitchen table, tucked away in an alcove. He smiled, remembering the card games they'd play after dinner — and the bickering and accusations of cheating that usually followed, sometimes with cards and dice spilling to the floor when a tussle broke out over the whole thing. But peace was always made once the dozens of pies and desserts were laid out. Probably just left them too stuffed and tired to fight.

Now, his mom and dad were down in Florida. Uncle Bill and Aunt Janice were in Arizona. Aunt Karen and Uncle Ben had both died, within two months of each other, incredibly. Most of the cousins had scattered across the country. It was a shame no one was around to keep the beautiful home in the family, with its stained glass windows, ten-foot ceilings and all those gleaming hardwood floors.

Selling it hadn't been easy. The place had been on the market for a year. He'd probably be able to make a faster deal selling a boat in the desert. It was hardly the perfect timing to have an expensive old home on the market. His folks thought it might help if someone were living there to oversee things. He was glad for one last opportunity to stay there. Spending it with Rachel was an unexpected treat.

But he couldn't shake the nagging feeling that while things would end, they wouldn't end well.

*****

Rachel kicked off her shoes and scooped up Hijinx. "Can you believe he didn't want to come in for a drink? Isn't 'come in for a drink' guy speak for 'action?'" She curled her legs underneath her, angry that she was too wired to sleep. The date had gone much better than she'd expected — until it's abrupt end.

She got up and flipped open her laptop, settling on the couch with a hot cup of tea to resume work on a logo design. It wasn't due for a week, but as a freelancer, she'd learned to get work done when she had the time. And here she was, alone after her first date with time on her hands.

What's he up to? It was certainly a different tune from the night before. Unless she was just so jaded by all those bad matches in the past she couldn't spot a nice guy right in front of her.

She was ready to climb into bed, when Lindsey called. "What are you doing, Rach?"

"I'm headed for bed." It was eleven.

"Aww, it's still early and Tyler and I are out with Luke. He's been talking about you ever since the wedding. We could double date!"

She wasn't ready to reveal the news that she had a new 'boyfriend.' She'd only met him yesterday, and Lindsey wouldn't buy it. "Sorry, girl. Not interested."

"I know what you said about not dumping

any more guys, but come on. Are you never going
out with another guy again? That's crazy. Luke's
handsome, rich and a foreigner. The trifecta of
men. What's the problem?"

"I said I was taking a break. But I met
someone interesting yesterday."

"Hey, that doesn't sound like a break. I'll
tell Luke maybe some other time. Talk to you
soon!" She hung up before Rachel could protest.

She lay awake for a few hours, playing out
the ways this unorthodox relationship could go.
And hoping he really would call the next day.

Thankfully, he did. She didn't realize how
deep and sexy his voice was until she heard him
on the phone. It was guys like him who must
have inspired phone sex, she thought.

"Would you like to go to the park and rent
a rowboat? I'll bring a picnic for lunch. What do
you say?"

"Sounds like fun." In all the years she'd
lived here, she'd never done that.

He picked her up and she sucked in a
breath when she saw him again, like maybe she'd
imagined how handsome he was. Nope. He was
hot.

She was more excited for their date than
she figured she'd be. She thought it'd take a while
to get on board with this ludicrous plan. Didn't
seem so ridiculous now.

They spent a few hours on the tiny lake in
the park, talking about everything. It was like a
microwave dinner version of a date. It was
strange, knowing this was all going to come to

end. It really took the pressure off.

When they finished their ride, he spread a blanket on the ground and knelt down, opening the picnic basket. "I'm trying out of a few new recipes on you. Keep in mind, I'm not formally trained yet, so go easy on me."

But the food was great: chicken salad with tarragon on homemade bread, Pinot Grigio, sugared grapes and a fruit tart.

The food was reason enough to stay with him all summer. "You're in trouble if I gain weight."

He popped one last bite of fruit tart in his mouth. "Don't worry, I'll still love you, sugar plum."

"No, you still have to dump me, remember?"

Frowning, he brushed off his hands. "Right. Well, we don't have to talk about that all the time, do we?"

She shook her head. She didn't want to think about it either.

They spent the rest of the day doing goofy stuff—swinging on the swings, zooming down the slide. They found a miniature golf course and she destroyed him.

But again, he dropped her off at home with a chaste kiss at the door and no pressure for more.

They grabbed a movie in the middle of the week, and she made dinner for them Friday night. Usually by the fourth date, she had a list of at least a dozen reasons that things weren't working out— different politics, bad manners, a voice she couldn't stand to listen to, or some other defect that took each guy out of the running.

But with Drake, she was doing the opposite, creating a running mental tally of all the reasons it *was* working—his humor, his soft lips, his interesting perspective on life. There was only one thing that bothered her. He was taking his time making a move. And it was happening again, as he made his way for her front door around eleven.

"Hey, how about dinner at my place tomorrow?" he asked. "I'd love to show you Grandma's house."

She tipped up on her toes and gave him a kiss. "I'd love to. I'll see you at six." Maybe for the first time in her life, she was the one who was going to have to make the first move.

*****

He was juggling three different pots on the stove when the doorbell rang. He wiped his hands and dashed to the door.

Rachel's eyes were wide as she stood gazing at the big front porch. "I can see why you wanted to spend the summer here. It's incredible. And I haven't even gotten inside yet."

"Come in. I can't wait to show you everything." He was thrilled she liked it so much.

"Gorgeous," she whispered, her eyes sweeping the room.

"I know. But it's more than that. It's all the memories. When I'm here, I don't feel like she's gone." Without thinking, he reached for her hand.

She looked up at him and smiled. His heart gave a jolt. Shit. He expected to have fun with her this summer, but he didn't expect to have feelings

192

for her — two weeks into it.

He led her into the living room, and she inspected every detail with genuine interest.

"Let me go check dinner while you look around."

She nodded, while grazing her fingers across the ornate fireplace mantle.

The lamb was perfect, and the risotto was almost finished. He drained the asparagus as she wandered into the kitchen. "I've been so distracted by how beautiful this place is, I missed how great everything smells."

"We'll be ready to eat in just a few minutes. Let me show you the rest of the place." He gave the risotto a quick stir and turned it off.

They walked into the hallway and stopped in front of the curved staircase. "When Grandma wasn't looking, we used to slide down the banister. I fell off once and broke my wrist, and from then on the banister was heavily policed. All the cousins were mad at me."

She ran her hand across the polished wood. "Can I try?" she asked.

"Sliding down the banister?" He laughed. "Sure."

She laughed and raced up the stairs. She flung her leg over the railing and slid down.

He caught her at the bottom. "Well done." His arms were looped around her waist and he wasn't sure how much longer he could indulge his patience.

She turned to face him, and he knew he couldn't put off their kiss again. A real kiss, not just a good-night-had-fun peck. He wanted her

more than anything. Tracing his fingertips along
her jaw, he raised her head to him. "How do you
feel about kissing on the fifth date? Long overdue,
I'd say."

"So, what were you waiting for?"

"I wanted to be sure you were on board."

"I've been on board for a while."
Tightening her grip on his shoulders, she gave
him a coy smile. "But kissing in your Grandma's
house? Is that allowed?"

"Now that I'm in charge, it's encouraged."
He brought her mouth to his, and their kiss
ignited every passion in him. He lowered her
onto the stairs and hovered over her, kissing her
softly. But she took a fistful of his shirt and pulled
him onto her.

"Yeah?" he said.

"Yeah." She kissed him, running her hands
across his back and his mind spun, imagining all
the different ways this could play out: on the
stairs, up in his bedroom, on the floor under the
chandelier.

But before things got out of control, he
pulled back. He didn't want to scare her off if
they got too close, too soon.

"What?" she asked.

"Are you sure? We have all summer."

She shook her head. "No, all we have is the
summer. Why waste any more time?"

Truth was, he didn't want to fall for her.
He had to go home in less than two months. But
looking down at her, with her hair splayed on the
steps, her pale skin glowing under the soft light
coming from the chandelier, there was no way he

could resist. He held out his hand and pulled her up. "Let me show you the bedrooms."

*****

What the hell just happened? They'd finally made it down to dinner at midnight, but she was too carried away to taste the food. And she was far too spooked by her feelings to spend the night. She dropped into her own bed at 2 a.m. and pulled her kitty on top of her. She stroked his soft fur. "It's probably because I haven't been with anyone in a while," she confided. "It wasn't really him so much. It was pent up frustration, is all." She nodded in the dark but heard the doubt in her own words.

And she tried to deny how incredible it had been.

Really, really incredible.

Rachel was in trouble. She was so spending so much time with Drake, she wasn't bringing in as much work. They decided to pack a year's worth of a relationship into their two months and even squeezed in a weekend getaway to the Cape.

A month into it, he drove her out to an empty field and laid out a blanket so they could watch the stars. "This is nice. What's the occasion?"

"Tonight's the night I tell you why I don't do long distance."

"Just like you promised." She was impressed he'd remembered. She'd thought it was a joke at the time.

They curled up on the blanket and kicked off their shoes. She dug her toes in the cool, soft grass. He looped his foot around hers. "Look, a shooting star." He pointed to a bright streak in the sky. "We're out here five minutes and see a shooting star. That's pretty lucky." He grabbed her hand and kissed it.

"So, I'm waiting."

He pulled her closer. "Technically we're in public. But I'm game if you are."

She nudged him with her knee. "For the story. The long distance story."

He sighed. "It's not meant for everyone, that's for sure."

She looped her finger around one of his curls and twirled it. "I've never tried it myself. What happened?"

He closed his eyes. "I became like one of the guys you dumped."

She sat up. "Oh, no. I don't think I want to hear this."

He patted her thigh and pulled her back down so she was lying on her side next to him. "No charges were filed, don't worry. No, I just became really suspicious, and really needy. We'd spent so much time together, and then she was just gone. And every time I couldn't reach her, I wondered what she was doing. She thought I was checking up on her, but I really just wanted to be part of her life still. Then I drove up to surprise her."

Crickets chirped as she waited for him to continue. "I guess that didn't go well."

"Nope. Knocked on her door and some dude answered." He shook his head. "I just don't think you can be a couple when you're not physically

196

together in the same place. So that's why this is going to end." He kissed her head. "Even though this has been awesome and fun, I need to remind you that I'll be leaving at the end of the August. And then it's over. Really."

Her throat tightened, and she could only nod. "I know. But there's still a month left and you could end up driving me crazy and forcing me to break up with you first." But she knew it wasn't true.

She poked him in the chest and he grabbed her finger and kissed her knuckle. "I'll do my best to keep you happy."

And she knew that *was* true. She folded her hand in his and watched the heavens, trying to convince herself everything was going to be all right. Because she thought she could smell of whiff of heartbreak on the breeze.

"So when am I going to meet this mystery man of yours?" Lindsey asked as they shopped for shoes during her lunch break. Lindsey thought she needed a new pair of do-me-now stilettos. Somehow, the heel on her last pair had snapped off in an escapade involving the elevator at Tyler's office building. Rachel had stopped her mid-story, certain she didn't need *all* the details.

Rachel set down a pair of red sandals. "He's not a mystery man. He's just someone I'm seeing. It's not serious." But her heart protested that line.

Lindsey examined her profile as she stood in pair of six-inch silver heels. "Good, because Luke is still asking about you."

"He's not really interested. I think with

him, it's a case of want-it-cause-I-can't-have-it syndrome." She sighed. "And guess what. He can't have it. Sorry to bust your double date bubble." She picked up a pair of open toed slides.

"Well, make sure this guy doesn't fall too hard. I don't think witness protection hides women from their crazy exes."

"It's not going to be a problem this time. He's leaving town in a month."

Lindsey raised an eyebrow. "Not if he's crazy about you, he's not."

"Sometimes people can't change their plans."

She handed three boxes of sex-worthy shoes to the salesman hovering nearby. "If you mean enough to him, he will."

*****

Drake's chest felt tighter, the closer the clock moved toward the open house his realtor had scheduled for noon. His purpose this summer was to sell the house and get out of dodge and on with his life. Somehow, his plans had changed.

Rachel finished vacuuming his living room. He planted a big kiss on her lips. "Thank you. I couldn't have gotten this ready myself."

She looped her arms around his neck. "Are you nervous?"

He nodded. "On the one hand, I really want it to sell. On the other hand, I hate to think of it leaving the family. Doesn't seem like there's a happy ending here." He had the same feeling about the two of them. He really liked her. It was becoming more than the summer fling he'd promised. If he weren't going to be leaving at the

end of the summer, he wouldn't want this to end.
Hell, he didn't want it to end now. But he was
going back to Philly for school and he'd never
change his stance on long distance relationships.
    She was watching him. "I can see it bothers
you." She snaked her hand under his t-shirt,
swirling her fingers in his chest hair. "The
realtor's coming in half an hour. Let's get out of
here and see if I can help you forget about this for
a while."

    Lying in her bed, with Hijinx snoozing in a
patch of sun on the cream rug, Drake did the math
in his head. They had three more weeks together.
How the hell had the summer flown by? And
how the hell was he going to leave this behind?
He tightened his squeeze around her waist, and
she wrapped her hand over his as it rested on her
smooth belly.
    "We don't have a lot of time left together," he
said quietly.
    "I know." Her voice was empty and flat, like
a glass of soda left out from a party overnight.
    They watched the shadows of the tree outside
her room dancing on the floor. "Are we going to
wait until the last minute to end this, or would it
be easier for you now?" he asked.
    She sat up. "No, don't put this on me. You're
breaking up with me like you promised." She
squeezed her eyes shut. "You do it whenever you
want to do it."
    "I don't want to." He kissed her shoulder.
"But I will."
    She ran a hand through her blonde waves and

sighed. "This was probably a stupid thing to do."

"No. It was the best thing I've done in a long time."

She nodded. "Then let's not talk about it again until you're ready to end it."

"Fair enough. Let's get dressed, see how the open house went and go out for dinner and celebrate."

"Celebrate what?"

"Either I have a buyer or I don't and I can find good reason to celebrate both of those options."

The open house was well attended, but no offers came out of it. His mother and father weren't too worried. The mortgage had been paid off, but there were still property taxes to be paid. "Maybe we could rent it?" Drake mentioned on the phone with them.

"Who's going to want to rent such a big house? And I don't want to risk someone damaging the place. We'll just cross our fingers and hope for the best," his mother said.

"You bored out of your skull up there?" his father asked.

Drake smirked. "No, it's good. I'm fine." He wasn't going to tell them about Rachel, because why bother? It would only get his mother all riled up for another lecture on the missing grandchildren in her life. "I'll keep you updated if there's any interest."

He wandered into the kitchen, with plans for making a divine lasagna. Rachel had mentioned it was her favorite. Filling up a pot of water, he frowned. He liked cooking for her. He liked doing everything with her. Would she ever consider moving to Philadelphia?

He lit he burner on the pot and shook his head. *No.* They had a deal and she seemed to want to stick to it. Maybe it was time to slowly back off. Stop seeing her every day.

But that plan went down the drain the next morning. "I'm going to delay some of my projects so I can spend more time with you," she told him.

They spent another perfect day together. This time, they ended up at her house. And as they were drifting off to sleep, he heard himself whisper, "I love you." He hoped she didn't hear it. Love wasn't part of their deal.

He got dressed early the next morning when the sun was just a blush in the sky.

She sat up in bed, "Where are you going?"

"I've got some stuff to do at the house."

"Like what? Can I help?"

Just tell her now. "I'm packing up to go back home. Every day, I'm getting in deeper, and it's not going to get any easier to say goodbye." He pressed his eyes shut. "So I'm going to say it now. Goodbye, Rachel."

She was silent, and with each passing second he was worried he would take back the words.

"You're breaking up with me." Her soft, hurt voice shattered him.

"Like I promised."

She looked down at the bed, fingering the edge of the sheet. "I understand."

He stared at her, but she wouldn't look at him.

He wanted to rush to her, hold her, tell her it was a big mistake.

But it wasn't. It was his only way out of this without causing even more damage.

He walked over to her, pressed his lips against her head and said, "You're fantastic, Rachel. I hope you have a really great life."

He heard her sob as he reached the front door. But he walked out, because if he went back he might never leave.

*****

Rachel was glad she'd postponed some of her projects. She was too depressed to work. If hospitals admitted heart break cases in the ER, she'd be a code blue. She knew she'd fallen for him, but she'd had no idea how hard.

Hard enough that she even agreed to go out with Luke, hoping that would remind her how ghastly men could be.

But that date—which involved too much wine on her part, and too much boasting on his part—only reminded her how wonderful Drake had been.

She tried to work, but she wasn't inspired. Nothing made her happy and she finally decided to call her mother for some good old-fashioned advice.

"Do you love him?" her mom asked, after Rachel filled her in.

She sighed. "Yes. But he doesn't want to do long distance."

"What's keeping you in Springfield? You work from home. You could do that anywhere."

She opened her mouth, but no great answer

came to mind. "I've got another three months on my apartment lease."

Her mother laughed. "And a lifetime of love waiting for you, it sounds like. Take a chance. That's what I had to do after your father died. It was hard. Harder than you can imagine. But then I thought of the alternative—a lifetime alone. What will your life be like without him?"

Rachel nodded to herself and struggled to swallow. "Thanks, Mom." She hung up and was ready to call Drake and talk it over. But she worried she'd chicken out and come up with a hundred reasons it wouldn't work. If she didn't get in her car and drive to him, she wasn't sure she could pull it off. She twisted her lips and then grinned. Showing up to surprise him might wipe away the memories of the girl who broke his heart when he did the same thing. *It's time to rewrite history.*

She called her landlord on the off chance she could get out of the lease early. Turned out, someone had come looking for an apartment a few days earlier. If she could get out in two days, the landlord would let her out of her lease.

She stored her furniture in her parent's basement, and then packed up Hijinx, her computer and her clothes. She googled Drake's address, programmed it into her GPS and hit the road.

She rehearsed several different versions of her speech on the drive down, but wasn't satisfied with any of them. Hopefully, seeing her stand in his doorway would say everything.

She sat in the parking lot of his apartment

building for at least fifteen minutes before getting the courage to rap on his door. After a few strange looks from a lady walking her dog, she decided she better go in.

After making sure Hijinx was secured in his carrier, she went inside and found apartment 3-C. She rang the bell and stepped back.

No answer. She frowned. She hadn't counted on this. He didn't have a job and he wasn't in school yet. Where was he? She rang again and knocked, hoping he was taking a nap. But still, no answer.

A man came out of the apartment next door and seemed surprised to see her there. "Are you looking for Drake?"

"Yes. I guess he's out."

The guy scratched his head. "Actually, he moved out."

Her jaw dropped. "Where did he go?"

"Where ever he was over the summer. Springfield, Mass, I think."

*****

His parents would probably give him hell for pulling out of culinary school, but he'd only lost his $500 deposit. Going after the woman he loved was worth so much more than that. He could go to school anytime. But a girl like her was once in a lifetime. He thought about calling her but didn't because he knew she'd try to talk him out of it. Showing up to surprise her would be worth everything.

He tried to shake away the bad memories from a similar trip, when he'd gone to surprise Kimberly. But this was different. He had no doubt she'd be alone, even though they were no longer together. If he knew Rachel like he thought he did, she was still just as miserable as he was. And that reassured him this was the right thing to do. He knew Rachel. He really knew her and loved everything about her.

After nearly swiping the guardrail in his rush to pull into the parking lot, he ran to her door. He knocked, but there was no answer. The shade on her front window was open, so he peeked in. His stomach lurched. The place was empty. She was gone.

Impossibly, it was an even worse feeling than seeing a guy on Kimberly's doorstop. He walked in circles, uncertain what to do. Where had she gone? He pulled out his cell to call her, but she didn't answer. *Damn it!*

At least he had a place to stay. He drove to his Grandmother's house and kept trying to call her, but no answer. He sat at the kitchen table and stared out the back window wondering if he'd just seriously screwed up his life for no good reason.

*****

Making the trip twice in one day wasn't her idea of fun. But she had to find him. Damn her lousy cell phone battery for conking out. What would he think when he discovered she wasn't at her place? Would he turn right around, too? Or maybe he hadn't come for her. Maybe it had to do with his grandmother's house. Maybe when he dumped her, he'd really meant it.

She swore to herself and wondered what she'd do next. When she finally got back to Springfield, there was only one place he could be.

She pulled into his grandmother's driveway at eight o'clock and took her first deep breath in hours. His car was there; he was home.

Poor Hijinx was meowing in the back seat. She freed him from his carrier and scooped him up in her arms. Her fingers trembled as she stroked his fur. What if Drake hadn't come back for her? What if this all had been a huge mistake?

She rang the doorbell and was relieved to hear footsteps coming down the stairs. When Drake opened the door, his face was pale and taut. Then he saw her. He pulled her into a hug while Hijinx meowed loudly. "You're really here?" She heard herself crying. "What happened? Why did you move?"

He led her into the hallway and closed the door behind her.

Hijinx jumped from her arms and disappeared into the dining room. Drake kissed her before she could explain. "I don't care where you went. You're here now. That's all that matters."

She laughed away her tears, wiping her cheeks with the back of her hand. "I was in Philly."

"What?"

She nodded. "I was miserable without you, so I broke my lease and came to be with you. It doesn't matter where I work." She shook her head and looked up at him. "I should have called. But I thought it was just better to get in the car and do it, before common sense intervened." She narrowed her eyes at him. "But why are you here? School starts in a week."

He kissed her forehead. "I missed you like

crazy. I pulled out of school. I can go again some other time, it doesn't matter. But you do."

She hugged him tightly, smelling his familiar scent, relishing the warmth of him against her cheek. "Well, I'm glad we've got that all sorted out. But what now? I broke my lease. We've got nowhere to stay."

He picked her up in his arms and headed for the stairs. "I think Grandma would be even happier to know I found true love than started culinary school."

She swallowed hard and stared at him. *Love?*

He nodded and climbed the stairs with her in his arms. "It's true. I love you. And I dumped you once. I won't be doing that again."

She laughed and leaned against his shoulder. "Good. I won't let you. But what happens when someone buys the house?"

He set her down in front of his bedroom. "Let me talk to my family. Living here with you would be a crazy dream come true."

Two weeks later, Rachel was dragging Drake to McGinty's to prove to Lindsey that her boyfriend was a real, living, breathing guy.

They approached the bar, and Drake gave her a nudge. "Check out the bartender's shirt."

She looked over and laughed at the phrase on his shirt. It read: 'I'm taken.'

Drake kissed her. "I'm getting one of those for you so you don't have to fight off the men looking to dance with you next time you're out alone."

They settled on a pair of barstools, and saw Lindsey and her boyfriend walking through the door…with Luke in tow.

She thinks I'm bluffing!

Lindsey saw her, and her eyes widened. She rushed over and kissed Rachel's cheek, then whispered, "He's hot! Is this for real?"

Rachel nodded. They made their introductions and told the crazy story of how they both moved out and missed each other.

Poor Luke was busy scanning the bar for new prospects.

"So now that we're homeless, we're planning to buy the house Drake's grandmother owned," Rachel said.

Drake squeezed her shoulders. "My realtor wasn't that disappointed when we took it off the market. She thought I belonged there all along. Her fiancé is even going to fix the roof at a nice discount."

The group chatted for a while, and Rachel was certain she'd finally convinced Lindsey this was the real deal, and she could send Luke packing for greener pastures. From the way he was staring at the dance floor, it appeared he already had someone in mind.

Rachel felt a tap on her shoulder. "I guess Great Aunt Mildred's love crystals worked."

"Brianna!" She hugged her cousin and introduced her to the group.

"I wonder how many other people hooked up after the wedding. Aunt Mildred wanted to spread the love, so she had the table seating and decorations set up with a feng shui love flair."

I winced. "I didn't take the crystals."

"Really?" She looked disappointed, then

shrugged. "Well, I guess it doesn't matter how you find love, as long as you find it."

"Very true. And you never know when you're going to find it."

"Hey, we found it when we promised each other we wouldn't," Drake said.

Brianna smiled. "I was at a wedding once, and the bride and groom were step brother and sister."

I laughed. "Now that's a small world."

Luke gestured to a tall blonde woman dancing in the crowd. "I think I found my very own happy ending right there." He pointed to the dance floor. "The hot girl, right there."

A dark-haired girl fishing a cherry out of her Coke spun around on her stool with wide eyes. "Are you Australian?"

"Yes, why?"

"You don't by any chance have a yacht, do you?"

He raised his chin. "Not yet. But my father does."

A devious smile unfurled on her face. "Let me introduce you to her." She hopped off the stool and pointed to the blonde woman. "I'm the hot girl's friend."

Rachel raised her glass. "To love, where ever and how ever it finds you."

About the Author

Lisa Scott is a former TV news anchor who now enjoys making up stories instead of sticking to the facts. She works as a voice actor and putters around in her koi pond and garden in upstate NY.

Go to ReadLisaScott.com to learn more about works in progress and the inspiration for her stories.

Look for more *Flirts!* collections including *Beach Flirts!, Holiday Flirts!, Fairy Tale Flirts!, Wedding Flirts* and *More Flirts!*

Find her on Facebook at Read Lisa Scott and sign up for her newsletter on ReadLisaScott.com to get the latest information on new releases.

Made in United States
Troutdale, OR
05/11/2024

19780288R00130